Rescuing the Lawman

(Christmas Rescue Series)

Cheryl Wright

Copyright

Rescuing the Lawman

(Christmas Rescue Series)

Copyright ©2020 by Cheryl Wright

Small Town Romance Publications

Cover Artist: Black Widow Books

This is a work of fiction. Characters, places, and incidents are a figment of the author's imagination.

Any resemblance to actual events, locales, organizations or people living or dead, is totally coincidental.

This book was written by a human and not Artificial Intelligence (A.I.). This book can not be used to train Artificial Intelligence (A.I.).

Dedication

To Margaret Tanner, my very dear friend and fellow author, for her enduring encouragement and friendship.

To Alan, my husband of almost fifty years, who has been a relentless supporter of my writing and dreams for many years.

To You, my wonderful readers, who encourage me to continue writing these stories. It is such a joy knowing so many of you enjoy reading my stories as much as I love writing them for you.

Table of Contents

Chapter One

Somewhere outside Alsburgh, Montana – 1880

Bethany Lancaster stayed right where she was – on the floor of the stage coach. The fact it lay on its side meant nothing to her, she intended to remain quiet and calm until help arrived.

When the shouting began, she knew they were in trouble. When the bullets began flying about… it was then she dropped to the floor. Unfortunately the only other passenger, a rather rotund man who was visiting his grandchildren, wasn't quick enough. His lifeless body lay across her, concealing the fact she was still alive. It probably saved her. His heavy weight also pinned her down to the point she couldn't move.

He was a friendly man, and had chatted about the grandchildren he had never met and his daughter he hadn't seen for over five years. He had noted it would probably be his last visit, so he'd intended to make the most of it. Little did he know.

A tear trickled down Bethany's face at the thought of it all.

They were going about their business, bothering no one. And now three people were dead. At least she believed they were. Her assumption the driver and guard were dead was likely correct since no one had come to check on her. She estimated she'd been there for some two hours now but she really didn't know. It could have been far longer.

Her senses heightened due to her dire situation, Bethany heard the sound of horses before they were even close. If the robbers had come back to retrieve what they couldn't carry earlier, she was doomed. Her heartbeat kicked up, and sweat poured down her face. She said a silent prayer to be spared. If she wasn't to be saved, then she wanted a quick death.

As the sound moved closer, panic hit and blackness overtook her.

"What a blasted mess!" The voice was distinctly male, and seemed rather unimpressed. "You two stand guard. The last thing we need is to be attacked. Keep alert everyone."

"Driver's dead," a different voice said. "So is the guard. Looks like they didn't stand a chance."

Bethany's breathing quickened but she couldn't find her voice. These men didn't seem to be the robbers, and may even be her saviors. So far no one had looked inside the toppled stagecoach where she lay with dear old Mr Carpenter's body across hers.

Without warning, the door to the coach flew open and a shadow lay across her. "Dear Lord, it's a massacre in here." The first voice stood close by, and Bethany dearly wanted to shout to him, to tell him she was alive. But whether from shock or something else, she couldn't utter a word.

"Pete." The shadow moved away and she found herself sobbing. Was she going to be left here to die under the weight of Mr Carpenter? She was beginning to go numb from the weight of him. If she could only move, even slightly…

From having a dead weight on her, she suddenly felt free, and Bethany knew she was dead. That sort of weight was enough to suffocate a person, and apparently, that's exactly what happened. At least her prayers were answered and her demise was relatively quick at the end.

"This one's still breathing! Someone help me get her out!" The shadow was there again. She strained to open her eyes, but it was so difficult. It took all her strength, all her energy, and she simply couldn't manage it.

Bethany felt as though she was floating on air, and resolved herself to going to her heavenly home. The Lord had beckoned and she had no choice but to answer his call.

"Miss! Miss!" She felt her cheeks being slapped, and not gently. She tried again to open her eyes, but couldn't manage it. Suddenly she was drenched with cold water and her eyes flew open.

"What the devil?" She opened her eyes wide and sat up. "How dare you?" She stared into the face of the evil creature who had doused her with water.

He grinned down at her. "Nice to see you, Ma'am. For a minute there, we thought you were dead too."

He reached out and shook her hand. "Hunter Bancroft, Ma'am. Marshal Hunter Bancroft. Welcome to Alsburgh."

"Bethany Lancaster," she said quietly, not feeling at all welcome.

Before she knew what was happening, Bethany was sharing a horse with the irritating marshal who had saved her life.

"What's the verdict, doc?" Marshal Bancroft asked.

Bethany sat on the side of the bed in the doctor's clinic. He'd given her a good checking over, and a clean bill of health. She had scratches here and there, and some cracked ribs from the weight of poor Mr Carpenter, but Doc Shilling said she was virtually unscathed considering the situation.

"I'm fine," she said, scampering off the bed and onto the floor. When she lost her balance, the fearless marshal came to her rescue. Again.

He held her by the shoulders to steady her and stared down into her face. "You sure don't look fine," he said, giving her the once over. "Apart from anything else, you're white as a ghost."

Bethany followed his gaze. He was right – she was a mess. Apart from the fact her clothes were torn and ruffled, she was covered in blood. No doubt from Joseph Carpenter. He was such a lovely man, decent and caring, and he didn't deserve to be killed. Perhaps worst of all, he didn't get to meet his grandchildren, and they would never know what a wonderful man he was.

Her eyes filled with tears and her head swam. The marshal's grip on her tightened as though he knew what was about to happen. "Miss Lancaster?" His voice came as though from an echo chamber and despite trying to stop the inevitable, she fainted.

She felt the support underneath her as she was gently laid back onto the doctor's table. "I thought you said she was fine, doc?" Bethany heard the irritation in the marshal's voice and tried to sit up in her stupor. He held her in place. "Stay right where you are," he told her, annoyance clearly in his voice.

From somewhere on the other side of the room the doctor spoke. "It will be shock," he said, then coming out of nowhere, waved smelling salts under her nose. Bethany was abruptly and suddenly wide awake. Her eyes flew open and she stared up into the bluest eyes she'd ever seen. She was surprised she hadn't noticed them before, but a lot had happened over the past few hours. Eye color was not something she often took notice of, especially when it came to strange men.

Not that she thought the marshal was strange. Oh no, that's not what she meant. What she meant was…she wasn't sure what she had even been thinking. Her head was still fuzzy and she was still a little light-headed, even after those wretched smelling salts.

He stared at her.

Marshal Hunter Bancroft stood there staring down at her. His face was blank, totally blank, as though she meant absolutely nothing to him. How could a man drag a person trapped underneath a dead body and not feel something for them? Apparently it was possible, because the marshal looked at her like she imagined he'd look at a loaf of moldy bread.

"We found your belongings," he suddenly said as though that was foremost on her mind. She nearly died while being attacked by outlaws, and he was concerned about her belonging? Heck, *she* wasn't worried about her belongings!

"Thank you," she said quietly. What else could she say? *I really don't care?* Here he was, believing himself to be kind and helpful when she couldn't possibly care any less about material things right now. She was alive and in one piece and that was all that mattered to Bethany at that very moment.

"At least we found what appears to be your belongings. We collected your reticule from the stagecoach too; it's in the Marshal's Office with the rest of your things." He indicated with his thumb and Bethany assumed it was down the street somewhere. She tried to sit up, but he held her there. "I'll bring them to wherever you are staying." He glanced across at the doc who didn't look too sure about her going anywhere.

"I, I have no where to stay," she said meekly, not sure what she should do. "I came out this way looking for work. I had no specific plans."

The doc frowned and the marshal scowled. "You came all the way out here with no plans of any sort? What sort of fool woman are you?" Marshal Bancroft bellowed.

Bethany cowered. Briefly. Then she sat up and stared him down. "The sort of woman who is homeless and penniless after her father died and everything was left to her selfish and useless brother. That sort." She climbed down off the bed and scurried out the door, leaving the marshal staring after her.

Hunter stared after the woman he'd rescued from the overturned stagecoach. "Ungrateful…" he began, then took a deep breath.

He twisted suddenly as the doc spoke. "She's in shock, Marshal. Give her time."

Hunter pushed back on his hat and scratched his head. "I don't think I'll ever understand women," he said under his breath.

"Maybe if you courted one and married her you might," the doc said, grinning at him. "Then again, perhaps not. Fifty years I've been married to my Martha, and I still can't work her out." He chuckled as he straightened the bed, and began to tidy the consultation room.

Hunter stared out the door, trying to see where the young woman had gone, but he couldn't locate her. "Thanks Doc," he said, waving over his shoulder as he left the clinic.

He glanced about the main street of town, but couldn't spot her anywhere. *Where did the darned fool woman go?* Alsburgh was no place for a single woman to wander about alone. It wasn't a bad town compared to others around here, but they did have a few thugs that had to be pulled in line from time to time. And despite the good time girls at the saloon, he still had to save some of the more innocent women from being harassed by those louts.

He straightened his shoulders and cracked his neck. It had already been a difficult day. Retrieving bodies was never an easy task, especially when you knew some of the victims. Elmer Chadwick had been driving the stagecoach from here to Ellensburg for as long as Hunter could remember. He had planned to retire in another six months.

Sure he was rough around the edges, but he was a nice fellow. Do anything for anyone, and he sure didn't deserve to die. It had been more than a year since they'd had a stagecoach robbery. Likely because nothing of value was ever transported to these parts. That made him pause. Did someone transport something valuable, gold perhaps, that he was unaware of? He frowned. He did not like being kept in the dark.

Three people had lost their lives because of this robbery. It could have been four, but for the grace of God. Bethany Lancaster was lucky to be alive.

That thought brought him back to the task at hand; finding the frustrating Miss Lancaster.

He strode to the mercantile and stuck his head inside. She wasn't there. He went to the hotel, but they'd had no strangers book in, so he checked with a few other businesses but she was nowhere to be found. Then he realized she had no money as her reticule was in the Marshal's Office. The more he thought about it, the more likely it was he would find her there.

Standing outside his office, Hunter pulled off his hat and stared through the glass panel. She was nowhere to be seen. His deputy sat at his desk, and on noticing the marshal, indicated the jail cells. He quietly opened the door to see the sassy Miss Lancaster laid out, sound asleep on one of the beds in an empty cell.

"Well, I'll be darned," he said under his breath.

The deputy grinned at him. "I didn't have the heart to send her away," he said. "She told me she had nowhere to stay."

"What the heck am I supposed to do with her?" He let out a slow breath.

Deputy Martin stood. "What about Nancy's? At least for a day or two," he added.

Hunter rubbed his roughened chin. "That might not be such a bad idea." He pulled her disheveled belongings out from a corner cupboard and began putting them back into her case. He held up some unmentionables and grinned.

"How dare you?" Bethany Lancaster shouted. He quickly put them behind his back.

She swiftly went from sitting on the side of the bed to standing beside him. "Give it to me," she demanded, and Hunter could see the anger written all over her face. He slowly brought his arm around to the front, but held his arm out so she couldn't reach. He wasn't sure what it was about this woman, but he sure got a kick out of riling her.

"Give me the wretched thing," she demanded, then quickly put her hands to her mouth.

Hunter stared down at her. She was a feisty little thing, and darned if he didn't like it.

Chapter Two

Thanks to the marshal, Bethany was settled into Alsburgh's only boarding house. Nancy Richter had owned it for over ten years, she'd said, and so far she'd had no trouble. Bethany took that as a warning. Marshal Bancroft told Nancy her story, and the woman was very caring. She even arranged a hot bath. Something Bethany had no intentions of refusing. Apart from being covered in a dead man's blood, she was aching all over. While she bathed, Miss Richter made her a hot cup of tea.

The towels were a little thin, but right now anything was appreciated. Tomorrow she would start looking for a job. Would a town of this size even have anything available? She would do just about anything at this point. Not that she was totally devoid of cash; she still had a handful of dollars, and that should get her through for a week or two. It was pure luck the robbers didn't get her money. If she and her reticule hadn't been stuck beneath Mr Carpenter, she was certain they would have taken it.

There was a tap to the door. "Are you nearly ready, Miss Lancaster?" a quiet voice asked. "I have your tea ready."

It wasn't a demand, and Bethany appreciated that. She'd dealt with demanding people most of her life, and it was time for that to change. "I'll be right out," she called back. She'd been in that bath for so long she was beginning to look like a wrinkled prune.

She hadn't brought many clothes with her anyway, but most of what she did bring had been ruined when the coach overturned. The stage coach robbers undoubtedly rode over her belongings, totally uncaring whether they were damaged.

Bethany stepped out of the tub and pulled a towel around herself. She felt so much better. And cleaner. She quickly dried her hair, then dressed. Feeling more human now, she headed for the kitchen.

Nancy Richter glanced up. "Oh, you look far better now. Not so disheveled and grubby. Did you enjoy your bath?" She smiled at Bethany, knowing full well she did.

"It was the best thing ever. After several days on trains and stagecoaches, I was aching all over."

"Sit down and enjoy a cup of tea." Nancy placed a hot mug in front of her, then added a plate of sliced orange cake. "Do you like cake, my dear?" she asked in a motherly way. It reminded Bethany of her own dear mother who had departed this earth many years ago. And now Father was with her. His death was far too raw. The moment his funeral was over, Bethany had packed up as many of her belongings as she could fit in her luggage, and left.

With her brother taking over the business, and Father's will leaving her absolutely nothing, she left. Joseph had no intention of giving her even one cent, despite him offering her a job. A job with no compensation. The absolute cheek of the man! She had trained alongside Father for years. Learned the trade, and was among the best in the county. Because she was born female, it meant absolutely nothing. Her inheritance was stolen from beneath her.

Emotion began to swell and she almost choked on her tea.

Joseph only wanted her there to teach him the family business. As if that would work. Joseph was lazy and didn't care one iota about the family business. Money was the only thing he cared about. Father should never have allowed for Joseph in his will. He'd never worked in the business despite constant requests, and had been waiting for Father to die for years. There was absolutely no doubt in Bethany's mind that Joseph would sell the business to the highest bidder the moment the opportunity arose.

She considered staying and appealing the decision, but an unmarried woman such as herself had no chance of winning that battle.

Bethany leaned back in her chair and sipped the tea. It was sweet; just how she liked it. The cake was moist and full of flavor.

"You've been through a lot," Nancy said quietly, watching her carefully. "How are you faring?"

"I'm fine," she said with a meek smile. The truth was not what people wanted to hear when they asked that question, and Bethany had no intention of giving it to her. "I'm sure after a good night's sleep I'll be even better." She continued to sip, and stared at her hostess over the rim of the cup. "The cake is good," she said honestly. "Did you make it?"

"Oh my goodness, no," Nancy told her. "I got it from the bakery in town." She scowled then.

"Is something wrong, Miss Richter?"

"Oh, do call me Nancy, my dear." She placed her mug on the table. "What's wrong is the bakery may end up closing. The baker's assistant recently married and left him. Now he has no one to help." She stared at the orange cake on the fancy plate with the gold edging. "That would be an absolute tragedy."

Bethany wriggled about on her chair, her eyes opened wide. Could it be true? She dared not believe it, but decided to ask anyway. "Is he looking for another assistant?" she asked quietly.

Nancy stared at her, then her mouth changed into a slow grin. "Oh my dear girl," she said excitedly. "Can you bake?"

"I am a qualified baker, and I can cook," Bethany answered. "My father owned a bakery back in Cedar Rapids."

Nancy interrupted her. "Iowa? Oh my goodness, you've traveled a very long way!"

She continued as though the other woman hadn't spoken. "When he died recently, the business went to my lazy…" She took a deep breath and held it for a moment, then let it out slowly. She stared down into her mug. "My brother owns it now."

Nancy rubbed her hands together. "This is so exciting! I can't wait to introduce you to Oscar Devlin. He will be as excited as I am."

Somehow, Bethany wasn't so sure.

Bethany tied her hair back, and placed her bonnet on her head. She looked down at her gown and shoes, and made certain she was presentable. First impressions were everything, and today they were even more important.

If she didn't leave a good impression on Oscar Devlin, he wouldn't give her the job. She ran her hands over her gown and straightened up. It was now or never. Nancy had been positively beaming at the news, but Bethany knew it was for selfish reasons. The woman wanted her fresh bakery goods supply to continue.

Bethany needed the job to survive.

Her heart was pounding at the prospect of having to prove herself to a complete stranger. It was something she'd never done before, and she moved quickly to the kitchen where she knew Nancy was waiting.

"Oooh, this is so exciting," Nancy said, pulling her bonnet down over her head. "Let me look at you." She walked around Bethany, checking her out. "Perfect," she said. "Shall we go?"

It was the last thing Bethany wanted to do, but she really had no choice. Marshal Bancroft had paid for a week's board in advance, brushing her objections aside. She'd told him she had money, but was embarrassed to admit it was very little. In the end she'd had no choice but to accept his gift. It seemed nothing to him, but to Bethany it was everything.

She would be sure to pay him back when she was able.

They strolled down the main street, Nancy pointing out the businesses as they passed them. "The mercantile is over the road, the butcher next door, and the bakery is a few doors further along." She was the most animated Bethany had seen her. The woman was obviously very proud of her town. "There are a few empty stores, as you can see. It's always a pity when a business closes down."

They crossed the road to the bakery, and she got a far better look of the diner and the shoe shop. There was also a tailor, although that store was fairly small.

They stood outside the large space which was the bakery. She wanted to watch for a minute or two and get a feel for the place. "That's Oscar," Nancy told her, pointing to a middle-aged man wearing round spectacles. "He took over when his father died a few years ago."

Bethany swallowed. She should have been doing the same thing. Joseph didn't know the difference between a bread tin and a cake pan. Why would you let someone with absolutely no knowledge of the business take over? At the very least, she should have been made part owner. But Father was one for traditions, and tradition demanded only her brother take control of the bakery.

She grinned. How was that working out for him?

She immediately felt bad for her vicious thoughts, but knew they were well placed. Joseph had demanded she work for him with no remuneration, which left her with no other option. She had to flee.

"Are you alright, my dear?" Nancy touched her arm, and she came back to the present.

She nodded. "Sorry, I was lost in my thoughts." They began to make their way into the bakery, but were stopped by a familiar figure.

"Good morning, ladies," the marshal said, nodding, then went on his way before they had a chance to respond.

Nancy grinned. "He's a fine figure of a man," she said quietly. "If I was a few years younger, I'd pursue that young man." She nudged Bethany. "He'd be perfect for you."

"He's arrogant," Bethany snarled, then stopped herself. He'd been kind to her, and helped when no one else had. She tried to put the vision of her undergarments dangling in his hands to the back of her mind. "But he was very kind to me," she had to admit.

"Of course. Our marshal is a lovely man. He'll make some woman a wonderful husband some day." She stared pointedly at Bethany.

"Shall we go in?" Understanding Nancy's reference, she wanted to go inside and get this over and done with.

"Good morning, Mr Devlin. I would like to introduce Miss Bethany Lancaster to you."

He glanced up, and adjusted his spectacles. "Nice to meet you Miss Lancaster."

"Likewise."

When nothing more was said, and Mr Devlin stood there expectantly, Nancy continued. "Miss Lancaster, Bethany, is a trained baker. I thought you might…"

He rubbed his hands together in glee. "Ah, thank you, Miss Richter. Do sit down Miss Lancaster, and we'll have a chat, shall we?"

Elation was written all over his face, and Bethany felt sure the job would be hers.

Nancy had long left them, and Bethany was put right to work. "I've been struggling since Mary-Lou resigned," Oscar Devlin said. "We'll make this a trial, shall we," he said with a smug look on his face. He knew very well she had no choice but to agree if she wanted a chance at the position he was offering.

"Tell me what you want me to bake, and I'll do it," she said, somewhat reluctantly. She wanted to work here, that was definite, but was he going to use her like her brother Joseph had tried to do?

"Shall we start with an orange cake?" He indicated a group of cupboards behind the counter and oven. "You'll find all the ingredients and pans in there."

Bethany stood and he reached for an apron, handing it to her. "Mary-Lou was the best baker I've ever had. Let's see if you can get even close."

She knew exactly what he was doing – he wanted to compare her baking with that of his former employee. It grated that he was doing that, but perhaps the man wanted to see how she performed under pressure. Well she would show him.

"My recipes are in there," he said, indicating a drawer under the counter.

Bethany waved him away. Every recipe she'd ever used was stored in her memory. Between her and her father, they'd come up with some very unique formulas over the years. Joseph would be quite disappointed when he went looking for them. Serve him right for being such an…

Ladies did not think that way, her mother's voice in her head reminded her.

She pulled a large mixing bowl out of the cupboard, six rather battered cake tins, and all the dry ingredients she would need. The remaining ingredients could be found in the icebox, and she removed them, ready for use. Mr Devlin stood back and studied her as she worked – it was a little nerve-wracking, but something she had to endure.

The bell over the door tinkled, and Bethany glanced up. The marshal strolled toward her. "Got yourself some help, I see," he said, acknowledging her but not addressing Bethany.

Mr Devlin scratched his head. "Perhaps. This is a trial."

"A trial for a shop assistant?"

Oscar Devlin grinned. "Miss Lancaster is a fully fledged baker," he said proudly, and her heart fluttered. Now all she had to do was pass the test.

She'd been there nearly two hours now and her cakes were cooked and cooled. While she waited, she familiarized herself with the layout of the bakery, and found where everything was stored. She made some pastry while she'd waited, and six apple pies were currently in the large oven. Her potential boss was impressed. At least she hoped he was.

Finally it was time to prove her cooking skills.

Bethany placed one of the cooled orange cakes onto a wooden board and sliced through it, cutting it into slices that could then be sold if Oscar Devlin so desired.

If her cakes met his expectations.

There was every possibility they did not, since her predecessor was apparently the best around these parts. She had to remember she was the unknown element in Alsburgh. Her reputation did not precede her like it had back home.

He sat at the small table where he'd interviewed her, a mug of coffee in front of him. He'd poured tea for her. Bethany took a restoring breath. This could be a defining moment for her. She carefully carried the slices over to the table on a white platter and placed it in front of the man who could decide her future. She then placed some small plates next to the platter.

He glanced up at her in anticipation. "Well, the moment of truth has arrived," he said. "Mary-Lou made the best orange cake I've ever tasted. We'll see if yours measures up."

She placed a slice on the shiny white plate and waited. "For goodness sake," he said, a little agitated. "Sit down. You're making me nervous."

She quickly sat. The last thing Bethany needed was to make *him* nervous. She was nervous enough for the both of them.

She watched as he swallowed down a mouthful of coffee then lifted a slice of cake to his mouth. Her heart pounded. Suddenly the door to the bakery swung open.

"Is that orange cake ready yet?" It was the marshal again. And he was grinning. She'd forgotten Mr

Devlin had invited him to come back for the taste test.

"Your coffee is on the counter."

She watched as the marshal grabbed the mug of coffee then sat down. The suspense was killing her; every moment delayed gave her cause for concern. She wanted to know if she had the job. Needed to know. If not, she would have to canvas the other business owners in town.

Each man lifted her orange cake to their mouths. Time seemed to go slowly as she watched them. She was terrified at that moment, and didn't dare try the cake herself in case she was left disappointed.

They each took a bite. She watched as they closed their mouths and simply allowed the flavor to flood their senses. Every moment that followed seemed like a lifetime. They said not one word, and it bothered her. Worried her.

She snatched up a slice of the citrus cake – she couldn't wait any longer. Bethany needed to know for herself. She shoved the cake in her mouth. Very unladylike she was certain, but she could wait no longer.

It was bliss. Easily the best batch she'd ever made.

She smiled. She couldn't help herself. Then saw the grin appear, first on Oscar Devlin's face, then that of the marshal. They both snatched up another slice.

She let out a long breath in relief.

"Wonderful! Even better than Mary-Lou." Oscar Devlin smiled at her.

The marshal grinned. "I have to agree. This is… words can't explain it," he finally said.

"The job is yours. When can you start?" Oscar Devlin asked.

"I thought I already had," she replied with a smile.

Chapter Three

It had been a long hard day. It felt like Oscar Devlin had worked her into the ground. The truth was, Bethany was still trying to recover from her long journey, and then her dreadful experience with the stagecoach robbers.

Not having an assistant had been difficult for Oscar Devlin. He was relieved to have finally found someone he could trust to uphold the quality, he told her. Her father had never had that problem with it being a family business. She wondered how Joseph was faring. With few qualified bakers in the area, she was certain he'd be selling up soon.

Serve him right for treating her so shabbily.

When she thought her day was about to get easier, Deputy Simpson entered the store. "We have one for tonight thanks, Oscar." He was gone as quickly as he'd arrived.

She frowned. What on earth was he talking about. She was about to ask when her silent question was answered.

"That's one prisoner we need to provide for," Mr Devlin said. "We provide the marshal with a meal too. He doesn't look after himself as well as he should." He scratched his head. "Goodness knows why – a lot of people rely on him."

He reached into the ice box. "Steak for the marshal, sausages for the prisoner," he said as he grinned. "Start preparing enough vegetables for two please, Bethany."

Between them they had an appetizing meal ready in no time. The two meals were added to a tray, and two buttered rolls added. Mr Devlin added a slice of Bethany's apple pie for the marshal, then placed a cotton kitchen towel over the tray.

"Can you manage that?" he asked her, indicating the filled tray.

Bethany lifted the tray. She'd carried far heavier in her father's bakery. This was nothing compared to the twenty-pound bags of flour she'd often moved from the storage room to the bakery. "I'm sure I can manage," she said.

Mr Devlin opened the door for her, and pointed in the direction of the Marshal's Office. She headed straight there. Now if only she could get through the door at the other end.

On arriving at the Marshal's Office, Bethany could see she was in trouble. The tray was big and cumbersome. If she let go of the tray to open the door, it would topple sideways, but if she didn't, the food would be cold. The only option she had was to put the tray on the ground, open the door, then pick it up again.

She was about to do so when the door suddenly opened. Marshal Hunter Bancroft stood in front of her, staring down into her face. She couldn't help but stare up into his sparkling blue eyes. "Well, hello there," he said, and her heart fluttered. "Let me take that from you."

Why was it that men always thought of women as helpless? Okay, so she was totally at the mercy of others when she was pinned under dear Mr Carpenter, but that wasn't the defining moment of her life.

Before she had a chance to be further annoyed, the tray was whisked out of her hands. Skin met skin, and she felt like she might swoon. He glanced at her. Then stared. Had he felt it too?

Don't be so ridiculous, she admonished herself. He was simply waiting for her to say something. "Thank you so much, Marshal," she said. "That tray was incredibly heavy." She couldn't help the sarcasm in her voice.

He continued to stare, then his mouth suddenly formed a grin. "I think I like you," he said, taking the tray across to a table in the corner of the jailhouse.

He pulled the kitchen towel off the food and stared. "Is this one of your pies?" He lifted the plate and brought it to his face, then breathed deeply, glancing sideways at her. "It smells delicious."

"It certainly is one of mine," she said. "Well, enjoy your meal. I'll be back later for the soiled dishes, I guess."

"The routine is that I bring them back when we're done. So I'll see you soon." He headed toward the cell with the prisoner's meal. That appeared to be her cue to leave.

Hunter leaned back in his chair. His belly was full, and for some reason he felt more content than he had for some time.

It wasn't the meal, Oscar had been feeding him similarly for as long as he could remember. But that pie… it was a totally different story.

Mary-Lou had been one of the best bakers the town had managed to have the good luck to find. If she hadn't married and moved away, she'd still be there. But then he would never have tasted the delicacies from Miss Bethany Lancaster. She was a bit of a firecracker, that one.

He wasn't sure if she intrigued him or annoyed him. One thing was sure, she set his heart on fire. He scratched the back of his neck. He'd got her hackles up when he'd thrown water on her back at the site of the robbery. He had to do it, there was no other way to revive her. Was there?

He shook his head. He was sure there wasn't.

That immediately put him on the backburner. She'd taken an immediate dislike to him. Not that he was enamored by her. Then there was that incident with her unmentionables. He had to admit he was being totally disagreeable by then. The poor woman had lost most of her luggage. Rather than taunt her, he should have been helping her in any way he could. Hopefully he'd made up for it by securing accommodation for her.

He stretched his long legs and yawned. It was time to return the tray of soiled dishes. He wasn't opposed to seeing Miss Lancaster again, even if she did tend to stir him up. He hadn't met a woman yet who could manage the weight she'd carried on that tray.

He scratched the back of his neck again. And yet… she didn't appear to be struggling. Hunter gathered up the plates and cutlery and placed them on the tray. The memory of that apple pie was foremost on his mind right now.

He felt bad that Oscar arranged supper for him most nights, but he wasn't taking charity. Oh no, that wouldn't do. He paid his way. Just because he didn't have the time to cook, Oscar had taken it upon himself to feed Hunter.

If he was truthful, time wasn't the issue. The fact he burned everything he tried to cook was more to the point. The town folks in their wisdom had tried to marry him off – on several occasions, but he was having none of it. What sort of life would the wife of a marshal have? If for no other reason than the worry of whether or not her husband would come home that night, there was the fact they often moved about.

Hunter had been in Alsburgh for several years now, and the townsfolk all seemed to be happy with him, and he hoped it stayed that way.

It was a quiet town, except for the occasional fight he had to break up. Sometimes he wondered if they did it to be thrown in prison for a day or two. The bakery's food was pretty good. Now that Miss Lancaster had arrived, he might be bogged down with prisoners vying for her meals.

He snatched up the tray and headed for the door, shoving his hat on his head. It was already dark outside, which meant it was almost time for the bakery to close. He hurried over the road and threw back the door.

When he glanced up, Bethany Lancaster stood at the counter. She was in the process of removing her apron, ready to go home. "I'll bring these back in the morning," he said, annoyed with himself for leaving it so late.

He turned to leave. "Please don't," she said as she stepped toward him. She tied her apron around her waist again. "I'll rinse them off now, and wash them properly in the morning."

He studied her. She didn't seem the type to do such a thing, but he had to take her word for it. "Alright then," he said. "As long as that is all you do."

She took the tray from him and headed toward the kitchen. "Where's Oscar?" he asked, then wished he hadn't. If the other man wasn't around, he was bringing attention to the fact they were alone.

Bethany turned to face him, and gave him a quizzical look. "He's in the storeroom sorting out supplies for the morning."

Hunter felt utterly relieved. He didn't know Bethany Lancaster, not really, and had no idea what she was capable of. Many a man had been tricked into marriage by women who had cried foul when it was totally untrue.

He stood in the doorway studying her as she rinsed the dishes. She pushed past him to return to the bakery. The slight contact sent a shiver through him.

He watched as she once more removed her apron, this time hanging up on hook behind the counter. She gathered up her things and headed to the front door. "Goodnight Mr Devlin," she shouted over her shoulder.

Her boss stuck his head around the door. "Goodnight Miss Lancaster. I'll see you in the morning." Oscar had a smile on his face – it was the first time since Mary-Lou had left that Hunter had seen him smile. Having help again had obviously changed his outlook. A week ago he was talking about closing up shop. That would have been a disaster for the town.

He held the door open and Miss Lancaster proceeded him out onto the main street, then headed toward the boarding house. He walked along side her.

"What do you think you're doing?" she snapped at him, staring him down.

He chuckled. "I'm making sure you get home safely." He should have realized she would object. She was that sort of gal.

They walked for a few hundred yards, then she stopped dead. "I am capable of getting myself home safely you know." This time she had her hands on her hips as she glared at him.

He knew better than to laugh. Now she was getting serious. "Well, we're almost there now, so no harm done. Besides, those robbers could be hanging around," he stared out toward the hills for dramatic effect. "And we would not know until they appeared. With you being the only witness…" He let his words drift away.

Perhaps he'd gone too far because now she looked terrified. "You don't think…?" She took a shuddering breath. "Am I in danger?" she whispered, and he felt like a total heel.

He stood in front of her and held her shoulders. "Did you see the robbers?" His words were firm, like he would use when interrogating a witness. He felt her shudder under his touch.

"No." The words came out as a whisper, and she sounded completely vulnerable. No longer the happy and carefree woman of a few hours ago.

He pushed his hat further back on his head. "Then you'll be fine. Besides, I'd know if they were still around. Believe me," he said firmly. "They are long gone."

She nodded then continued walking, but said not another word. He felt badly for scaring her, but it wasn't safe for a woman to be out walking in the dark alone. Especially when she was not familiar with the layout of the town.

They walked in silence, almost shoulder to shoulder. He had a sudden urge to put his arm around her, but was almost certain she would slap his hand away. A chuckle bubbled up his throat at the thought, and there was nothing he could do to stop it.

"What's so funny?" she demanded, hands on her tiny hips again.

"Nothing." Nothing that he could tell her anyway. If he voiced what he'd been thinking, she would surely slap his face. She might look frail, but Hunter was certain there was more to Miss Bethany Lancaster than it appeared.

"Here we are," she said, reaching into her reticule for her key. With the moonlight playing across her face, Hunter studied her. She had almond shaped eyes that called to him, and a pert little nose. Her lips were full and moist, and suddenly her tongue shot out and licked her lips.

It took all his restraint not to lean forward and kiss her. He shook himself mentally. It was ridiculous where his thoughts were going. He did not like her, and she sure as heck didn't like him, especially after that stunt with her unmentionables.

The door suddenly flew open and there stood Nancy Richter. "Evening Marshal. What brings you out here?"

His attention moved from the appealing lips of Bethany Lancaster to Nancy. "I was making sure Miss Lancaster got home safely." He touched the tip of his hat. "Well, I'll be saying goodnight to you ladies now."

As he turned to leave, Nancy called him back. "The kettle has just boiled if you'd like to say for a bit?"

He didn't have the heart to say no. Besides, Nancy Richter always had the best cake – straight from the bakery. "Well, thank you, Ma'am. I don't mind if I do."

He followed Miss Lancaster into the house, and at Nancy's request, made himself completely at home. He loved this little town.

Chapter Four

It was a busy day for Bethany. She'd offered to start early like she always did at her father's bakery. Oscar Devlin would have none of it. He was emphatic and said it wasn't right for the two of them to be together, alone in the bakery at that hour of the morning.

When she thought about it, he was right. She was after all, a single woman, and he was a single man. They were not that different in age. It had never been an issue before – she'd always worked with her father in the early hours.

He didn't think she was trying to put him in a compromising situation, did he? The thought made her shudder. She hoped he didn't think that was her intention, because what she wanted was to establish herself as a great baker and a good employee. She wanted to make herself indispensable, but didn't want to be too obvious about it.

What she'd seen so far of Alsburgh, she liked. It was a quiet little town, away from the hustle and bustle of the city, and the people seemed friendly enough. Marshal Bancroft however, had seemed more than a little rude at the doctor's office. Once he was through the door at Nancy's boarding house, he was a totally different person. Toward Nancy anyway.

When it came to Bethany, he was reserved and rather standoffish. That was fine with her. She wasn't interested in making friends here. She wanted to concentrate on working at the bakery and earning enough money to rent a place of her own. Maybe down the track, if she was frugal, she might even buy her own place.

She shook herself. It was rare for a woman to save that much money, even if she skimped and saved. Earning far less than men made it an impossible dream.

"Good morning, Miss Lancaster," Marshal Bancroft said as he entered the bakery. "Everything alright in here?" He craned his neck to see through to the kitchen area and the storeroom.

"We're fine," she said, a question on her tongue.

He saw right through her. "Doing my morning rounds," he said. "Unless something untoward happens, you'll have the pleasure of seeing me every morning around this time." He grinned and quirked an eyebrow at her.

The man was infuriating, and she felt like throwing something at him, but not something that would do harm. Bethany glanced about. She snatched up a kitchen towel and threw it across the room toward him. He ducked but it hit him square in the face.

Her aim never was that good.

"Hey," he yelled. "That wasn't nice. And this thing is wet." He made his way to the counter, a scowl on his face.

She wasn't sure if he was really mad, or joking with her. Standing opposite her on the other side of the counter, he pushed the kitchen towel toward her, then let it drop near her hand. He stared down at her, still scowling, and she studied him. It wasn't long and his face softened. Then his hand slipped along the counter toward hers.

His gaze did not falter. He stared into her eyes and Bethany found it hard to pull her gaze away.

"Miss Lancaster," Oscar said, strolling into the room. "Have you... Oh." He quickly returned to where he came from.

Bethany pulled her hand away. "Is there something I can do for you, Marshal?" she asked as though he was a complete stranger.

He looked hurt. "Not really. I'd best continue my rounds." He was out the door before she could say anything further.

Oscar Devlin ducked his head around the door. "Is it safe to come out," he asked quietly.

"Perfectly safe," she said, slight annoyance in her voice. "I was about to start the pastry. Six apple pies again?"

"Make it ten," Mr Devlin said. "Those pies were snapped up yesterday. We'll need to start thinking about Christmas soon," he said. "It's only a matter of weeks away, and the customers are already asking."

He was right. Father would have had his Christmas menu sorted by now. With everything else that had happened lately, it hadn't entered her mind. "I have an old family recipe if you're interested. It's a rich cake, passed down through generations. I guess it depends on your customers. Do they prefer cheap or quality?"

She stared at him for long moments, waiting for a response. He tapped his finger to his chin as he thought. "Some like cheap, but the majority of customers around here prefer to get a quality product."

"Oh, and puddings. Do you sell many of those?"

His face lit up. "Since Father died, I haven't been able to locate his Christmas pudding recipe. I think he kept it up here," he said, tapping his temple. "This time every year, I have nothing but complaints regarding the lack of puddings."

She grinned. Bethany felt as though she was meant to end up here. She grabbed a sheet of paper and made a list of the ingredients she would need. Mr Devlin, or Oscar as he was now insisting she call him, would ensure the necessary ingredients were available when she needed them.

Being the only bakery for miles around, the store was relatively busy. They took turns serving so they each had time to do their allocated baking for the day. Apart from her apple pies, Bethany made several orange cakes, which were a favorite with the locals Oscar told her, a few pound cakes, and two dozen blueberry muffins. The latter were sold individually.

He had set up a few tables recently, and had begun serving tea and coffee. It was a way to draw more customers into the bakery. His hope was it would bring groups of the local ladies together, and they'd buy more of the baked goods being offered before they left.

Apart from serving and baking, it was also her job to clean down the tables. It was not a favorite task, but had to be done. If it kept her in a job, Bethany was not going to complain. She was busy cleaning the tables when the bell over the door jingled. She glanced over her shoulder to see the marshal enter. It hadn't been that long since he'd been here, so she was surprised to see him again so soon.

He winked at her. Bethany stood tall. The man was beginning to annoy her.

But he was a customer, and we don't upset customers, she said under her breath. "Hello Marshal. What can I do for you?" She strolled over to the counter carrying a bucket of soapy water and a wash cloth. She washed her hands in the small basin against the wall.

His gaze burned into her back.

"For some strange reason, I'm quite hungry," he told her, trying to keep his expression serious. She saw right through him.

"Did you not eat breakfast?"

He straightened his shoulders and cracked his neck before answering. "I rarely eat breakfast. It's far too time consuming."

She scowled. "I find that rather hard to believe," she told him, then bit her lip. He was after all, a paying customer. For some reason she had to keep reminding herself of that fact.

"Can I buy one of those bread rolls," he asked, pointing to the basket of fresh rolls on the back counter. "What do you have to fill it?"

"Nothing."

He studied her. "Are you mad at me for some reason?"

She squirmed under his scrutiny. "No, why would I be mad?" Maybe because you felt you could take liberties by trying to cover my hand with yours, she wanted to scream. But she held her temper.

"I just thought…"

Oscar would be furious if she turned a customer away. "Oh, wait. I think we have a chunk of ham. Let me check." She opened the icebox and sure enough, there was a small piece of ham there. "I was right. Would you like some cheese with that?"

"Yes please, and a mug of coffee." She glanced up at him but said nothing. "Did I tell you I'm having it here?"

Of course he was. Just to annoy her no doubt. "Take a seat then," she said and went into the kitchen to prepare his food. Marshal Bancroft was seated at a table when she returned, his long legs stretched out under the table. He'd removed his hat, and it was sitting on a spare chair at the table.

"It looks good," he said as she placed the food in front of him. He threw some coins on the table, enough to cover his food and more. "Keep the change for yourself," he said with a smile. "A tip if you will."

Bethany was fuming. She wasn't penniless and didn't need his tip. If she said anything it would surely become an argument. It was as though he purposely set out to annoy her.

She went back to work while he ate in silence but felt his eyes on her almost the entire time. She wanted to hide in the kitchen, but with Oscar working in the storeroom, that just wasn't possible.

The marshal didn't seem in a hurry to leave. He'd placed himself in a position to see outside, and shared his gaze between Bethany and the main street. A number of customers had come and gone while he sat there indulging himself, and it frustrated her. She wasn't sure why.

There were other empty tables, so he wasn't stopping paying customers from sitting down to eat food. He wasn't blocking the way of customers entering the store either. She really didn't know why she felt so irritated by the man.

Except perhaps that he took liberties he had no right taking. Like displaying her unmentionables to the deputy. Like throwing water in her face. And presuming he was her protector when he was no such thing.

Finally, he pushed his plate away. The bakery was currently empty so Bethany moved toward his table and lifted the plate. His coffee mug was almost empty. "More coffee," she asked reluctantly. If she refilled his cup, he would stay longer, but it was Oscar's policy to refill at no extra charge.

He stared up at her, but didn't speak while he pondered. "I'd better not," he finally said, regret in his voice. "I need to check on the prisoner, and I still have more rounds to do." He stood and stretched himself to his full height. "Oh, that will be one for supper tonight. Do you need a hand with the tray?"

That really got her annoyed. "I am perfectly capable of carrying a tray with two meals on it," she said between gritted teeth. Bethany stormed over to the door and opened it, indicating for him to leave. In response he grinned.

"You have quite a temper for such a pretty little thing," he said, believing his words to be funny.

Bethany felt her back stiffen and it took all her effort not to shove him out the door. "Get out," she said quietly but forcefully.

He chuckled and then left. He glanced back over his shoulder and winked at her. The blasted man, he thought himself to be so darned special. In reality he was a nuisance. She slammed the door and went back to what she was doing.

Chapter Five

It was hard to believe she'd been here over a week already. The days seemed to fly.

Bethany was busy in the bakery, either cooking or serving, then at night, spending time with Nancy relaxing. That was after the marshal walked her home, much to Bethany's annoyance.

Marshal Bancroft had also taken it upon himself to visit several times throughout the day. Oscar said the marshal was sweet on her. Well she wasn't sweet on him. The man was arrogant and self-centered.

She glanced up as the bell over the door tinkled. Before she even checked, she knew it was him. She sighed. "Hello Marshal," she said. "What can I do for you?"

He must have heard the exasperation in her voice, because he studied her. "For one thing, you can call me Hunter." He grinned.

"Like I said, what can I do for you, Marshal?"

He scowled. "Why does it always seem like you're mad at me?" he asked as he stared into her face. "Am I really that bad a person?"

It was as though she'd slapped him – he seemed that upset.

"For one, I'm not a *pretty little thing*," she said quietly.

He grinned. "I beg to differ."

She tried to ignore his words. "I don't need your *tips*. I have a paying job." She waved her hands about, indicating the store.

"Fine," he said. "No more tips – noted."

"Last but certainly not least," she said with emphasis, "I am not weak. I can easily carry that meal tray when it is full."

He pushed back his hat and stared at her. "On that point, I do object. Women are not strong enough to carry heavy items."

Bethany felt her temper rising. "Is that so?"

"I stand by my words. Oscar," he called, looking for back up. When the other man appeared he made the same statement.

"Follow me," Bethany said out of desperation, and scurried into the storeroom with the two men following.

"You're out of your depth here," Oscar whispered loudly to the marshal, and Bethany couldn't help but chuckle despite her annoyance.

She walked toward the pile of flour. "See this," she said pointing at the bags. "Each of these are twenty pounds."

He stared at her. When she leaned over to pick one up, he leapt forward to help her. Then he stopped dead in his tracks. Bethany threw one of the bags over her shoulder. It was lightweight to her, she'd done it for so long.

He scowled, then suddenly grinned. "I guess you're not just a pretty little thing after all," he said.

Bethany put the bag back where it belonged, then shoved past him and back to the store.

She heard the two men joking on her behalf, and felt her temper rising. She thought she would make things better, but she'd only made them worse.

"I'm going for a walk," she told Oscar when the men stepped back into the bakery. She glared at Hunter and pulled off her apron.

There was far more to Bethany Lancaster than he'd first imagined. She had a lot of spunk, a smart mouth, and she sure had a temper. The man who got to tame that little filly had his work cut out for him.

The thought made him chuckle.

"What's so funny," Oscar asked.

"Miss Lancaster. Pity the man who has to tame her."

Oscar stared up at him. "I thought you were sweet on her? Have you changed your mind?" He pushed his spectacles up his face.

"I thought I was, but I'm not sure I want to deal with that temper of hers. I'm willing to bet she's accustomed to throwing things." He scratched the back of his neck.

"Not that I've seen. Not so far at least, but you push her to the limit." Hunter glanced across at him momentarily. He still had his eyes on the firecracker who had stormed out of the bakery.

"Makes me think you do like her," the other man said, a grin on his face.

He shook his head. "Not likely. Besides, having a wife is not a good move for a lawman. Far too much worry for the women folk. You know that."

He stared down at Oscar who was a full five inches shorter than Hunter. "Maybe she'd be a good wife for a baker," Oscar said, and that got Hunter's hackles up.

Scowling, he turned to the baker and Oscar backed off. "I was only joking," he said, hands in front of him.

"No you weren't." Hunter opened the door and headed toward a group of teenage boys who had congregated further up the main street. They seemed to be up to something, but he wasn't sure what. About ten of them stood in a group, pushing at something. It could only mean trouble of some sort.

If there was one thing Hunter didn't stand for, that was trouble.

"Right you lot, what are you up to?" They began to separate as he approached. Bethany stood there, an annoyed look on her face. Otis Jackson, the town drunk was holding her around the waist.

"We tried to stop him, Marshal," one of the boys said. "But he wouldn't let the lady go."

Hunter approached the man. He was usually a pushover. "You've had your fun, now let her go." His hand hovered over his gun, but Hunter hoped he didn't need to use it.

Bethany said something to her attacker but he couldn't hear what. Suddenly she stomped her heel on his foot and the man screamed. "Why you…" He jumped about, trying to hold his injured foot.

Hunter sprung forward and grabbed his arm, then began to drag him toward the jail.

"Are you alright," he called back over his shoulder.

"Of course, no thanks to you."

He gave her a small nod and forced himself not to smile. "Make that two for supper tonight," he said, and dragged the man away.

Bethany brushed herself off and returned to the bakery. Oscar rushed toward the door. "Are you alright? Come and sit down," he said, guiding her toward a chair.

"I'm perfectly fine. Stop fussing," she said firmly. "I need to dust myself down is all."

He threw her a tentative smile. "I see the marshal sorted Otis out."

"*I* sorted Otis out. The marshal did nothing to help. These ridiculous heels I am forced to wear do come in handy sometimes." She glared at him.

"I don't know about you, but I need a strong coffee. Can I get you one?"

Bethany considered him for a moment. He was only trying to help and she was not acting at all grateful. "Tea would be nice, thank you," she said. As much as she didn't want to admit it, she was rather shaken. If the teenagers hadn't surrounded Otis, it could have been far worse. If the marshal hadn't come along when he did, it could have been worse still. But she wasn't going to give him the satisfaction of telling him that.

"You stay here," he said as she began to rise. "You've had a scare. Stay here and calm down."

She did as she was told. He was her boss after all, and he was paying her to follow orders. At no point would she admit she was rattled.

No sooner than Oscar returned with their refreshments and the bell over the door tinkled. She knew before she saw him it was the marshal. She'd know that scent anywhere. He made it a point to get as close to her as he could, and the fragrance was growing on her. The man wasn't necessarily though.

"Hunter. Let me get you a coffee." Oscar jumped up and soon returned with a mug of coffee for him.

"I'm fine," she said before he'd even sat down on the chair he'd pulled out from the table.

"You don't look fine." He reached for the mug Oscar placed in front of him. "You're deathly white."

"He's just the town drunk. He's not dangerous." She was determined to not let the situation get on top of her. So why was she trembling?

Hunter reached out and covered her hand with his. He didn't say a word, just stared into her face. It was as though he'd read her mind. "Fine, huh? Then why are you shaking like an earthquake is rolling through the main street?"

"I've got stuff to do," Oscar said, suddenly pushing the chair back. Perhaps he thought he was intruding, but he wasn't.

Hunter totally disregarded him. "No, he's not usually dangerous, but he gets out of hand sometimes. He's never snatched a pretty lady before though."

She began laughing. "Has he snatched an ugly lady?" She couldn't stop herself from laughing, and eventually tears began to roll down her cheeks. He reached over and wiped them away with the back of his hands, then handed her the mug of tea.

She took a sip. Despite that, the tears continue to fall. She must look a mess. Not only was she dusty and disheveled, but now her eyes would be red and puffy. She stared at Hunter, and he stared at her.

"Let me take you home," he said gently. "You've endured so much lately."

She brushed at her cheeks and stood. "I'm not going anywhere. I have work to do." With that, she stood, gathered up the empty mugs and headed to the kitchen leaving Marshal Hunter Bancroft to stare after her.

Several hours later, Bethany was ready to leave. Her experience of earlier had finally hit her and she felt flat. But she couldn't leave yet.

No, that wasn't quite true. Her boss had tried relentlessly to get her to go home.

Hunter Bancroft had called in several times trying to convince her as well. He even wanted to accompany her home. But she would have none of it. She wasn't some weak wallflower who needed a man to make sure she was safe. She thought they'd both understand that by now, especially the marshal. Apparently not.

She prepared the tray for the evening meals. Three meals tonight. Not that Otis Jackson deserved to be fed, the rat. Despite that, she prepared three meals.

There was no leftover apple pie today, but she'd made peach cobbler earlier today for customer meals, and still had a large slice left. She dished it out for the marshal. Not that he deserved it. He had a smart mouth when it came to her, and Bethany was getting rather sick of it.

She conceded that wasn't really true. Whenever she'd needed him, Hunter had been there. He was a different person when he was in marshal mode. It was when he got personal – specifically with her - she had a problem with him.

Lastly she dished out the hot beef stew and dumplings with mashed potatoes and peas for three. She added three buttered bread rolls, and some cutlery. She covered the tray with a large kitchen cloth.

"I'll get the door," Oscar called as she headed out.

She glanced about before leaving. She shouldn't be worried, the man was locked up. As she approached the jailhouse, the door opened. Hunter held the door open and waited for her. He seemed please to see her.

"I wasn't sure if you would come," he said quietly. "I do look forward to your visits each night."

Visits? She was working, delivering meals. "Of course I came," she said, leaving the tray on the table where she left it every night. She removed the kitchen cloth and he leaned in.

"Smells delicious. Did you make it?"

"You think Oscar can cook this good?" She smiled, although she didn't feel particularly happy. She was still shaking from her earlier encounter.

Then she spotted him. The drunk was sitting on the bed, staring into space. "You! You lousy no good…" She lurched forward. How she thought she would reach him through the bars, she wasn't sure.

Hunter pulled her back. His touch sent shivers down her spine.

"Sorry Missus," Otis said. "When I'm drunk, I dunno what I'm doin'."

"Then don't get drunk." She shivered, and felt the tears bubbling up again. Hunter tightened his grip on her. "It's alright," he whispered gently, trying to calm her down. "Darn it, Oscar should have brought the meals over here tonight."

He led her to his desk and sat her down. "Let me sort these meals out, and I'll be back," he said pulling the cell keys out of the desk drawer. "You alright?"

She nodded, but he didn't look convinced.

He returned a short time later, and sat opposite her. "Eat your food," she said. "Before it gets cold. I have to get back anyway." She stood to leave. "I'm alright, I promise," she said and headed for the door.

"If you're sure. I'll be over to walk you home before you close up." She nodded and left without another word.

Chapter Six

As promised, Hunter arrived at the bakery a few minutes before closing time. He carried the tray of soiled dishes into the kitchen. "The peach cobbler was delicious," he said as he studied her.

Bethany seemed to be calmer now, and nowhere near as upset as she'd been earlier at the jailhouse. Otis was a problem for another day.

"I'll rinse these off and then I'll be ready."

There were no arguments about him walking her home tonight. It seemed Otis really had put a scare into her. He could totally understand that.

Dishes rinsed, she cleaned down the tray and put it aside, then pulled off her apron. Watching her was mesmerizing. Everything Bethany did, she did to perfection. It never looked like hard work; she tackled it head on and simply did whatever needed doing.

"Goodnight, Oscar," she called over her shoulder.

"Goodnight," he called back. "Don't forget to grab that extra orange cake on your way out," he reminded her, so she did. "Nancy loves orange cake."

"I think I'm ready," she told Hunter, placing the cake in her bag and taking her bonnet from the pigeon hole where she kept her belongings out back. He helped her into her coat.

"It's getting colder now. Make sure you rug up from now on. It won't be long and it will be snowing."

She quirked an eyebrow at him. "I guess it will," she said. "Christmas is not that far away."

Hunter opened the door and she made her way through ahead of him. "I'm starting on Christmas fare tomorrow," she told him as they strolled down the main street.

"That sounds about right." He loved Christmas with all it's festivities and color. Many of the business owners would begin putting up their trees and decorations soon. It helped to draw customers into their stores. No doubt Oscar would do it soon as well.

The only thing he didn't like about Christmas, was being alone.

"We're making puddings this year."

He glanced across at her. "Oscar hasn't done puddings since his father died."

She stopped and turned to him. "Did you know the recipe died with his father?" He didn't know that and told her so.

"I guess I'm just as bad. My recipes are all in my head, which is just as well because Father never wrote his down either."

"But your brother…"

"That's his problem." She almost snarled the words. "Back to puddings, the ingredients are due in first thing in the morning. If you're lucky, I might have some left for your evening meal."

That sounded far more enticing that it should. But he was getting fed up with eating alone. Well, apart from the prisoners that is. "Maybe we can have a meal together one night," he suggested and waited for her denial. He already regretted the words.

"That would be rather nice, I think."

Did he hear that correctly? Bethany Lancaster didn't reject his invitation?

"It certainly would. Just the two of us."

"I can make something special," she said looking rather thoughtful.

Let her cook for a night out with him? That would never do. "I will make a booking at the diner. Tomorrow night after you close up?"

"Sounds wonderful."

As they continued to walk, he slipped his hand into hers. A little cheeky, but he hoped she wouldn't mind. She stared at him momentarily, but didn't pull her hand away. He gently squeezed her hand.

It had been years since he'd felt anything for a woman, and Bethany Lancaster was the last person he thought he'd be attracted to. There was something about her that intrigued him. Perhaps it was the fact she got his hackles up. Or maybe that she let him get away with absolutely nothing.

He grinned.

"What's so funny?"

He dare not tell her what he was thinking, otherwise she might cancel their date.

That made him pause. *Was it a date?* He guessed it had to be. His heart did a little dance and he felt warm all over.

"Well, here we are," she said, reaching into her reticule for her key.

"I'm looking forward to our… supper tomorrow night," he said quietly.

She turned to face him. "I am too. It's a very long time since I've eaten out."

He stared down into her face. She no longer looked upset, or scared. She seemed more relaxed than she'd been since she arrived. She'd once called him her protector. Did that make her more comfortable?

At the time she'd sounded annoyed. Right now she looked as far from annoyed as she could get.

She stared at him. As though she was waiting for him to kiss her. Her eyes sparkled in the moonlight, and her tongue came out and licked her lips. It was his undoing.

Hunter cupped her face with his hands, and moved in to kiss her. She didn't push him away, and he took that as his cue to continue. Took it as permission.

Before he had a chance to do anything, the door unexpectedly opened. "I thought I heard someone out here. Oh!" Nancy looked startled to see them in that position. "Did I interrupt something," she asked with a grin.

"No."

"Yes."

They both spoke at once. Hunter grinned at Nancy, then winked. "I was just leaving," he said. "I wanted to ensure Bethany got home safe."

"Of course," the older woman said. "Especially after what happened today." Word got around far too quickly for his liking.

"Where are my manners. Stay for supper, Hunter."

"I've had supper, thanks to this wonderful lady, but I wouldn't mind a slice of that orange cake," he said, and Bethany pulled it out of her bag.

"Then come on in. The kettle is already boiling."

Hunter waited for Bethany to enter the boarding house, then followed suit, closing the door behind him. He wasn't sure where any of this was going, or even if it would continue, but the more time he got to spend with Bethany the better.

At least he thought so.

The more time they spent together, the more relaxed Bethany felt around Hunter. He seemed to have warmed to her as well.

He'd been a different person at Nancy's last night. He'd seemed comfortable and chatted away to the both of them. It was almost as thought they'd known each other for years. When Nancy dished up supper for Bethany and the other boarders, she handed Hunter a meal as well. At first he'd refused, but then accepted.

She couldn't help but grin. He certainly had a good appetite. "You do know he had a full meal not an hour ago," she informed her landlady. Hunter winked at her.

"He's a growing boy," Nancy said as though he was a teenager.

"You don't think he's grown enough?" Hunter was well over six feet tall and could barely get through the doorways as it was.

He grinned at her.

She liked this new banter they now shared. Before they just annoyed each other, but these days they seemed to understand each other better. Hunter was one of the few eligible men in town, but seemed to be one of the hardest to catch. According to Oscar, he was never really interested in settling down, citing his job as the biggest handicap.

Bethany could understand that. Being a marshal, or even a deputy, was dangerous work. If the robbers had returned when they'd rescued her, their lives could have been in grave danger. Just the thought of it made her feel ill.

They finished dessert and made their way into the parlor. "Sit down, Hunter and I'll bring you a mug of coffee," Nancy told him, not giving him a chance to refuse.

"You must be overloaded," Bethany said. "I still can't believe you ate a second meal." She sounded serious, but despite that, she smiled at him.

He studied her. "I'm a growing boy, you know," he said, almost laughing as he spoke.

She frowned. "Perhaps I'm not giving you enough?" She worried now. He was the sort that wouldn't complain, and would just take what he got. Her cheeks warmed at her embarrassment for not feeding him properly.

He turned to her. "It is more than enough," he whispered. "Have you ever said no to Nancy Richter?"

They both laughed, and Nancy walked through the door right at that moment. "What's so funny?" she asked, placing a mug of coffee in front of Hunter, then handing a tea to Bethany. Her cheeks warmed again.

Instead of answering, Hunter completely changed the subject. "I really must go when I finish this coffee," he said smoothly, diverting attention away from their earlier conspiracy. "I still have my nightly rounds to do."

"Well, I do appreciate you walking our Bethany home each night," Nancy said, taking a seat opposite him. "You never know who or what is out there."

He nodded then took a sip of his coffee, staring at Bethany over the rim of his mug. His eyes shone mischievously, and it took all her restraint not to laugh. Whatever would Nancy say?

Nancy began to add wood to the fire. "It is getting quite chilly at night," she said. Hunter took over the task, allowing Nancy to rest.

"I said that to Bethany when we were leaving the bakery," he said. "Soon Christmas will be here, and it will be colder still."

"You are right. I must organize for the young Jones boy to chop some more wood for me. He does a good job, and doesn't charge a fortune."

Hunter took his seat again and leaned over to Bethany. "The *young Jones boy* is almost twenty," he told her. "He's been chopping wood for the townsfolk for at least seven years."

She couldn't help but chuckle.

Suddenly he gulped down the rest of his coffee and stood. "As much as I'd love to stay, I have to go," he said. "I have rounds to do."

Bethany stood too, and walked him to the door. Hunter put his coat on, and opened the door. "I had a wonderful night," he said. "The best for a very long time. I'll collect you at the bakery as usual and we'll go to the diner."

"About that…"

He frowned at her. "Oh no you don't." he said quietly. "You're not getting out if it that easily."

Hunter suddenly stepped forward and cupped her face with his hands.

His mouth covered hers, and it felt like they belonged together. She moaned, an almost silent sound, but it was there. She leaned into him and they melded together. His hands went up her back, and Bethany felt she was right where she belonged.

He suddenly pushed her away. "I'm sorry, I shouldn't have done that." He stared down at her, annoyance evident.

She stared up into his face. "Why not?" she asked quietly, feeling a little disappointed at his reaction to what seemed a natural progression to their friendship.

"I had no right." He pushed back from her and turned to leave.

"What about tomorrow night," she demanded.

"It was always a bad idea," he said, then quickly disappeared into the night.

Chapter Seven

Bethany spent the best part of her morning making Christmas puddings. They were more time consuming than most other items she baked. Even using the largest pot they had, only four puddings could be cooked at one time, and each batch had to be boiled for hours.

Oscar had bought up all the calico available from the mercantile, and ordered in another ten yards. If they didn't use it all this year, it could be stored for the following Christmas. Assuming she was even still there.

The moment word got around, they'd been flooded with orders for puddings. There was only one way that could have happened – Hunter. No one else knew.

She'd had to set up an order book, and glancing through it, wondered how she would ever make enough puddings to fulfil the orders. Either she'd be making puddings virtually non-stop, or Oscar would have to buy at least one more large pot.

She would get *young* Tommy Jones to ask his mother to increase their egg order by at least five times. Bethany hoped the chickens could keep up.

Her arm was already aching from all the stirring she was doing.

She glanced up as the bell over the door tinkled. It was Hunter. That was all she needed.

"Good morning," he grumbled as though what happened last night was her fault. It wasn't.

She nodded but didn't speak, and continued to mix. "Sure," she finally said.

It really wasn't a good morning. For weeks he'd treated her like a leper, which had suited her fine. Then suddenly last night, he'd asked her out, kissed her, and dumped her all in a matter of hours. What sort of reception did he expect?

"I guess I deserve that," he said. "I came to tell you there are no prisoners for supper tonight."

She glanced up again and stopped momentarily. "Fine. Thanks." She was far from interested in small talk and wished he would leave.

He pushed his hat back on his head, fiddled with his gloves, and pulled his coat further around himself. It seemed like he didn't want to leave. "I also want to apologize."

"You know where the door is," she said abruptly, not interested in his explanations.

"Bethany…"

"It was your choice," she said, beginning to lose her temper. "Now please leave."

He stared at her, sadness evident on his face. "I…"

"Not interested," she said, then picked up the bowl and went into the kitchen. She didn't return until she heard the bell tinkle over the door as he left.

"Don't you think you're being a bit harsh?" Oscar knew something was wrong when she'd arrived this morning, and was sympathetic when he'd finally dragged it out of her. "The poor man has no idea how to treat women. He deals with criminals and thugs all day, and you expect him to be perfect."

He looked serious, but she wasn't sure if he was.

"Not my problem," she said, then returned to the bakery. She laid the four wet pieces of calico across the counter, sprinkled it with flour to form a thick white coating on the cooked pudding, then divided the recipe evenly. Once done, she pulled the sides up, tying each bundle with thick string. The events of last night ran through her mind. Had she done something to make Hunter suddenly change his mind?

No matter. Her opinion of him was correct from the start. He was arrogant, he was self-centered, and really didn't care for her.

If that's true, why does he walk you home every night? That voice in her head was unrelenting.

Hunter Bancroft cared about himself and his town. If something happened to her, it would be a blight on his reputation.

She dropped the tightly sealed packages into the boiling water and closed the lid. *Then why did he ask you out?* That's easy – because he wanted something different for a change.

She strolled back into the bakery. *Why did Hunter kiss you if he has no interest in you?* That was the most baffling question of all. She had absolutely no idea of the answer.

What she did know was she felt wanted when she was in his arms. When he was around, she felt protected too. She'd never felt that before. At Nancy's he'd been open, funny, and she was comfortable in his presence.

Perhaps Oscar was right. Maybe she was being too hard on him. Well, it was too late now. He'd acted like an ass, and now he had to live with it. Bethany placed ingredients in a fresh bowl. She would make carrot cake this time, and see how that went down with the locals. Oscar had given her virtually a free run on what she made, provided she fitted in some of the favorites his customers came back for time and again.

He spent most of his time creating his specialties – bread loaves and rolls – while Bethany did all the sweet products. Between them they were doing really well.

"Time for a break, I think." Oscar was a very generous boss. They seemed to have more breaks than she ever got working for her father, and she wasn't complaining. He put the kettle on and she finished mixing her carrot cake. By the time their drinks were poured, the cakes were in the oven.

She had her back to the door at one of the tables, when the bell tinkled. Oscar stood, grabbing his mug as he went. She instinctively knew it was Hunter. If she hadn't already been certain, she was now that Oscar left a mug of coffee on the table then made himself scarce.

She glanced up as Hunter approached the table. He sat without an invitation. That was his arrogance coming out.

"Do you mind," he asked once he was sitting and sipping his coffee. Too bad if she did – he'd already sat down and made up his mind to stay. "I'm really sorry about last night. I was totally in the wrong."

She glared at him. "Yes you were." She began to leave, but he reached out and held her hand.

"Stay. Please." His eyes begged her, and she didn't have the heart to refuse. Despite sitting down again, he didn't let go of her hand. It felt good, comfortable, and she didn't try to take it away.

"I know I've been hard to get along with."

"You think?" If it hadn't been so serious, she would have laughed.

He pulled his gaze away from her face and stared at their entwined hands. "I am not the easiest person to get along with, I know that."

He got that right.

"I hold myself at a distance from people I care for, because I don't know what is going to happen from one minute to the next." He stared at her as though she should know what he meant. "Take yesterday for example. Otis could have hurt you. Or even killed you."

She watched as he tried to compose himself, and she tried to swallow down her own emotions.

"He could have, but didn't," she told him quietly. "You wouldn't have let him."

Hunter took a large gulp of his coffee. "No, I wouldn't have, but you fixed the problem before I could." He grinned then, lifting the mood.

"I didn't know what else to do," she said. "I was scared, really scared. I knew he was drunk, I could smell it on him. The teenagers tried to entice him away, but Otis wouldn't budge." She closed her eyes then, trying to force the memory to the back of her mind, but it wasn't working.

Hunter squeezed her hand, then stood, pulling her up with him. His arms enveloped her and she leaned against him. There was only one thing on her mind, and that was the man holding her. He might be infuriating at times, but he was also very special to her.

The diner was near empty, which didn't upset Hunter at all.

The fact he'd been able to entice Bethany to still come after his stupidity of last night, amazed him. He'd acted like a teenager, and there was absolutely no excuse for it. He was a grown man, and should know better.

Only he didn't. If he'd taken the advise of the townsfolk over all these years, he'd have found himself a good woman and married her. Until now, no one had caught his interest. Now that she had, he had a hard time because she was up and down with her moods. One minute she was sweet as pie, and the next she lost her temper and was off like a firecracker.

It took all his effort not to grin. He did like the firecracker – sometimes. Other times she went way too far. He wasn't sure he could cope with that on a long-term basis. He frowned. *Who mentioned long-term?* Right now they were getting to know each other.

"Is everything alright?" Her gentle voice brought him out of his thoughts.

He glanced up. "Sure. I was just thinking, is all."

"I'm glad you changed your mind about tonight. The food here is wonderful."

"Yours is better," he said, sliding his hand across the table to hers. "But I wouldn't tell Martha that."

"What's that?" Martha Greenwood, owner of the diner, suddenly appeared beside him.

Bethany tried to hide her smile, but it didn't quite work. "I was saying the food is perfection," he said, trying to cover up his comments of before.

"It really is," Bethany said. "I really enjoyed your chicken pot pie."

Martha smiled. "You can come anytime you like, my dear," she said, then leaned in and cleared the table of their soiled plates. "Desert?"

"Can we have a menu, please?" Hunter said. The desserts were always good here, but again, not as good as Bethany's.

She shuffled away and returned soon after with a menu, then left them alone again.

"There's Cherry Cobbler," Hunter said, reading out the menu. "Apple Pie, Lemon Tart, Blancmange, or Bread and Butter Pudding."

Bethany screwed up her face at the last item, and it made him laugh. "I do love a good lemon tart," she said. "Bread and butter pudding is a good way to use up leftover stale bread!"

Clearly she didn't approve. It made him chuckle.

"It's true," she protested. "I would never serve such a thing in a diner."

Martha arrived again, took their order for two lemon tarts, then left them alone again.

"I'm having a great time," Hunter said after Martha was out of earshot. "I'm sorry about, you know." He didn't want to bring it up all over again. After all, it was totally his fault, and he didn't need reminding of that fact.

This time it was Bethany who reached for his hand. "I am too," she said. "Let's try to forget about the unpleasantness and move forward."

He nodded his agreement. It wasn't long until their desserts arrived, along with a strawberry that had been sliced and decorated with cream. Their hot beverages also arrived.

It had been a long time since Hunter had eaten here. With Oscar providing him with a meal most nights, he no longer needed to frequent the diner. He still liked to come in from time to time, if for no other reason, than to support Martha's business.

"If making so many puddings hadn't reminded me, I'd know Christmas was approaching," Bethany said.

Hunter was confused until he glanced about. There in the corner of the diner was a small Christmas tree. It was so small it was barely visible from across the room. Martha had made an attempt to decorate it, but hadn't gotten far. Or perhaps she thought it was enough.

Either way, it made him chuckle.

"Does Oscar put up a tree in the bakery? Or decorations?"

"Sometimes he puts decorations on the window. Can't say I recall ever seeing a tree there."

Bethany sighed. "I guess that's going to be my job from now on."

He felt certain she would enjoy doing it, but she was so overloaded with the onslaught of pudding orders right now, she probably felt overwhelmed. "I'm sorry about spreading the word on the puddings. I didn't realize you would be overloaded with orders."

She waved his concerns away. "We'll cope. Oscar is rubbing his hands together. He said the bakery has never been so busy."

"And all because of you."

"Perhaps. Or perhaps not. Anyone could have done the same thing."

That was just like Bethany, discounting the part she played. "Anyone else isn't here. You are, and you're doing a wonderful job. Oscar told me so himself, and that's high praise if ever there was."

She shrugged her shoulders as though she played only a small part in the bakery's success. "Shall we go for a stroll?" he asked. Bethany agreed.

They both stood and headed toward the front door of the diner. "Supper was wonderful, Mrs Greenwood. Thank you," Bethany said.

"I hear you're a far better cook than me," the older woman said, glancing across at Hunter. "I'm very pleased you haven't opened your own diner."

Did she overhear their conversation? Hunter hoped not – he had tried to be discreet. "You underestimate yourself," he said, trying to right a wrong. "The food was delicious. It always is." He helped Bethany into her coat, paid the account and they were soon on their way.

"Do you think she heard me talking earlier?" he asked almost the moment they were out the door.

Bethany grinned at him. "You're being oversensitive. I'm certain she didn't. In a town like this, gossip abounds, you know it does."

He sighed. "You're right. Tomorrow the gossipmongers will be talking about us. Instead of having supper together, we'll be courting, and soon to be married." He knew it was true. Small towns always had their gossips; there was no getting around it.

"Would that be so bad?" She had such a cheeky expression on her face, he knew she was teasing him. But she was right, it wouldn't be so bad being married to the firecracker standing beside him right now.

"Maybe, maybe not." He pulled his coat around himself, then offered his arm. "Where would you like to go? There's not a lot to see around here."

She finished fastening the buttons on her woolen coat, then linked her arm through his. "Wherever you think I may not have seen? Honestly, I don't know. But I miss the long walks I used to take in Cedar Rapids before Father died."

He could understand that. Cedar Rapids was far bigger than Alsburgh. It could be considered a large city, so there would be plenty to see. Mostly the town of Alsburgh consisted of Main Street where the majority of businesses were, and Chapel Street, which sat behind Main Street Lawn and was occupied by the church and the pastor's house. The rest of the town was mostly spread out beyond what was known as the city limits. Nancy's boarding house was one of those places.

"There's a real chill in the air tonight," she said, and visibly shivered. He stopped and began to remove his coat to put around her shoulders. "Oh no, I'm not that cold," she said.

He'd rather freeze himself than see a lady cold. "Only if you're certain. I'm used to the cold."

"I'm certain," she said firmly, and they continued walking.

She glanced up toward the mountains where fog was already forming around the peaks. "It looks so beautiful," she said as she gazed toward the very top.

"It is beautiful. We could go there one day. Just the two of us."

She glanced across at him, appearing a little coy. "Perhaps."

"Sunday after church?" If he made a specific time she was less likely to back out. "Do you ride?"

She studied him. "Yeah, sure. I ride." Her sarcasm was more than a little clear. It made him chuckle.

"Then I'll hire a buggy. We could have a picnic lunch straight after church if that suits you. It could be the last opportunity we have to go for quite a while. It will be snowing soon; as early as Monday or Tuesday going by previous years."

Her eyes danced in the moonlight and he was mesmerized. He couldn't see the color of her eyes in the darkness, but pictured her blue eyes with their mischievous glint.

"I'll bring a blanket," he said suddenly trying to pull his attention away from her face. "In case it's cold. We can use it to picnic on too."

She nodded her agreement, although he wasn't certain she was one hundred percent on board. "I'll provide the picnic food," she suddenly said.

"I was going to…"

"You supply the buggy, I supply the food. Fair is fair."

So that was it. They had a date for Sunday. Their second date. He nodded his agreement, and warmth flooded him.

Chapter Eight

Sunday couldn't come around quick enough for Hunter.

He arrived at the boarding house early enough to have breakfast with the other boarders. Nancy had insisted. If he was coming to collect Bethany, she'd told him the previous evening, then he needed to eat with them. He never said no to Nancy's cooking. Or Bethany's for that matter.

The aroma of pancakes and coffee drifted from the kitchen the moment he'd stepped through the front door. It set his mouth to drooling. Nancy directed him to the dining room where some of the other boarders were already seated.

"You're almost part of the family," Jonas Hedges told him when Nancy handed him a mug of coffee. The pair sat in front of the fire as they waited for the food to be served.

"I'm not sure I'd go that far," Hunter told the much older man. "Bethany and I are friends."

Jonas studied him. "If that's all you are, then you need to tell the young lady that. She seems rather besotted."

Hunter nearly choked on his coffee. That was the last thing he expected to hear. He and Bethany had become closer over the past weeks, there was no doubt about it, but besotted was not how he would have described their relationship.

Although if he was honest, he was becoming particularly fond of the town baker.

"She could do worse than you," Mildred Hanover piped up and told him. "Although truth be told, I wouldn't marry the marshal."

"Mildred," Jonas interrupted. "You *did* marry the marshal. Harry Hanover was one of the best we've had." He eyed Hunter. "Not counting you, Marshal."

"Exactly my point," Mildred said, waving her hands toward Jonas. "And look what happened to him. Shot dead by outlaws."

Hunter cringed. That was the last thing he needed Bethany to hear. But then again, he wasn't looking to marry her, was he? Since Bethany came along he hadn't felt the emptiness he'd felt before she arrived. He didn't feel as agitated either. He wasn't certain that was her doing, but he had to wonder.

"Good morning, Hunter."

Bethany's sweet voice broke through the gabble that went on around him. As he glanced up, the first thing he saw was her cheerful face. She wore a soft mauve gown today, and the color suited her. She'd swept her hair up and pinned it neatly at the back of her head. He far preferred it down, but she rarely did that, especially when she was working.

His heart thudded the closer she got to him. He stood awkwardly and almost stumbled on top of her. "Sorry." She was a vision to behold, and he was totally lost for words.

"Breakfast is served," she finally said, and ushered him toward the dining table. "You sit here, next to Mr Hedges."

The moment he sat down, Nancy refilled his coffee mug. "What can I do to help?" He felt like an intruder. All these lovely people surrounding him lived here. He was just the interloper getting a free meal now and then. But he'd come to look upon them as family, just as Mr Hedges had suggested. Having Bethany in his life had changed so much for him, he didn't even know where to begin.

"Marshal, would you like to say the blessing this morning?" It was Elizabeth West who spoke, better known as Lizzie by everyone in town. She and her husband were the original owners of the mercantile. He'd died a few years ago, and Lizzie had decided to sell up and retire. She enjoyed the company, she'd told him on more than one occasion, and she certainly seemed happy living here.

Nancy's Boarding House was more than somewhere to live, it was a little community all of its own.

As he glanced about, Hunter realized everyone was waiting on him, and he bowed his head as they all linked hands. "Lord, thank you for the bounty before us. Bless this food and these people. Amen."

Echoes of *Amen* could be heard around the table. Warmth flooded him, and something shifted inside Hunter. For the first time in his life, he truly felt as though he belonged.

As they left the church, Bethany felt light headed with anticipation. Today, along with Hunter, she would venture into the hills. She could only imagine the view from up there. Assuming they traveled to the top, that was.

She'd put together a picnic, and included some sweet items as well. She'd made a Christmas cake especially for today, packing four slices and leaving the remainder at Nancy's for the boarders there.

She'd picked tomatoes fresh from Nancy's garden, and made their sandwiches. One for her and two for Hunter. She'd already discovered he was a big eater, which wasn't surprising as he was a large man. You would think his size was enough to drive the criminals away.

The picnic basket was sitting underneath the blanket Hunter had brought along. Both sat on the back of the buggy waiting for the pair to return.

Bethany pulled her coat around herself and tucked her scarf down the front before securing the fastenings. Hunter had already told her snow was close, and he was right. It was icy cold outside, and although it was probably a good idea to postpone their trip, she knew it would possibly be the last opportunity for some months.

Hunter stood at the door chatting to Pastor Henry Kelly before finally slipping away to join her out the front. If it wasn't for her coat and scarf, not to mention her gloves, Bethany was certain she would have froze standing out there in the elements.

"Sorry," Hunter said, almost running toward her. "We were having a quick chat about the Christmas hampers."

"Hampers?"

"The ladies auxiliary put together hampers for our less fortunate, and do a special one at Christmas," he explained. "Those living further out of town often barely survive. The hampers make their lives easier."

That got Bethany thinking. "I'll talk to Oscar. Perhaps we can help in some way. I'd like to help, even if I do it alone. "

"That would be great." He helped her up onto the buggy and they were soon on their way. "It's getting chilly," he said soon after they'd entered the dense bushland, then pulled the blanket up around their legs. He slid a little closer to ensure they were both warm, her leg now resting against his, and Bethany didn't complain.

She was more comfortable than she should have been, and she thought perhaps she should move away. But frankly, she didn't want to do that. Hunter glanced across at her and as though he could read her thoughts, grinned. "Are you alright there?" he asked, then stared ahead again.

"I'm fine. Do you know where you're going?"

He frowned. "Of course I do. I ride up this way all the time. See that track," he asked, pointing to a barely visible trail that went off to their right. "If you follow that for about two miles, there's a rundown shack. Old Nellie Bridges lives there. I check on her every other week, more often when I can, to make sure she's still alive and kicking. She's eighty if she's a day and won't move into town."

To hear Hunter talk like this warmed her heart. How many other townspeople worried about Mrs Bridges? If she had to guess, Bethany thought not many. She would make it a point to bake something special for the dear lady in time for his next visit. Perhaps he'd even let her go along.

It wasn't long and Hunter pulled into a small clearing. She could hear a small stream in the distance. She reveled in the fragrance of the pine needles, many of which had fallen to the ground. He climbed down from the buggy and tied the horse to one of the bushes, then reached out for Bethany.

She shivered as his hands made contact with her waist, despite the thick woolen coat and gloves between them. The mere thought of his touch set her skin alight. She stared down into his face and she was filled with warmth. Never before had anyone made her feel this way.

He slowly lifted her down from the buggy and gently placed her on the ground, his eyes never leaving her face. "Bethany," he whispered, pulling her close against him. "I don't know how I ever survived without you."

Her hands went up against his chest, ready to push him away. Hunter leaned down and brushed his lips against hers then deepened the kiss, and all thought of deflecting him were gone. She melded into him, and her heart fluttered at the close contact they had.

Then suddenly he pulled away. "Sorry," he said gruffly. "I have to learn to control myself better than this. Being around you makes it difficult." He went around to the back of the buggy and pulled the picnic basket down while Bethany spread the blanket on the ground.

"It's a lovely spot," she said, ignoring his words. To acknowledge them was to concede the fact he'd kissed her and they'd both got carried away in the moment. She stepped closer to where the sound of water seemed to be coming from.

"Careful," he shouted. "It's slippery… there."

Before the words were out of his mouth, she landed on the ground. Hunter reached for her, pulling Bethany away from the slippery bank. "Well darn," she growled. "My coat is all muddy now."

He pulled her farther away from the edge, and checked the coat out, spinning her around, his hands on her waist. "It's not too bad," he told her. "A little bit of mud won't hurt you." His eyes glistened with the laughter that was bubbling up, and it changed her demeanor.

"I guess it is funny, provided you're not the one covered in mud." She grinned and his face softened.

"I don't know about you," he said after a moment or two, "But I'm getting hungry."

She began emptying the picnic food onto the blanket and his eyes widened. "Well, I won't say no to any of that," he said. "Especially the Christmas cake. When did you have time to make it?"

She grinned. "A couple of days ago, in between the puddings. I left the rest for Nancy and the boarders."

"I'm not complaining," he said.

Hunter reached for a sandwich at the same time she did, and their hands brushed. Bethany loved the thrill his touch gave her, but didn't know if she affected him in the same way. Should she mention it? Bethany decided it probably wasn't a good idea. She had no intention of embarrassing herself if he felt no such thing.

After they'd eaten, she poured them both a mug of water from the bottle she'd brought along. Then they went for a short stroll after packing up their picnic. "It's so peaceful here," she said quietly. "I could spend forever up here."

"You couldn't do that," he said. "Where would I get my supper from then?" He grinned at her, and her heart did a quick flip. Even when he was being silly, he made her feel good. He reached over and took her hand in his, then turned to face her. His hands cupped her face, and she stared into his eyes. She licked her lips and tilted her head back to allow him access to kiss her.

And that's exactly what he did.

The past week had been a busy one. Apart from making endless puddings, Bethany was determined to put together something special for Mrs Bridges. Hunter had declared he was visiting the dear soul after church, and she begged him to let her tag along. He finally agreed.

She made an orange cake and two chicken pot pies. She sliced up a Christmas cake, and wrapped several slices. She made a small Christmas pudding as well. She visited the mercantile and brought some scented soaps, a warm scarf, a pair of warm gloves, a lap blanket, and a small bag of apples. It wasn't a lot, but enough to make the dear lady know someone was thinking of her.

They collected the buggy from the livery after church, then went back to the boarding house where Jonas Hedges helped Hunter put together a small box of tools and some pieces of wood. He explained it would be for any repairs that might be needed. Nancy had invited Hunter to eat with them before they left for their big adventure.

Roast lamb was not something he had often, Hunter told her, but he certainly enjoyed it. Bethany had made two apple pies for dessert, of which he had two helpings. To his credit, he'd refused a second slice, but Nancy had insisted. And as he'd told her before, with a grin no less, you don't say no to Nancy.

By the time they left, they'd both eaten more than their fair share. Nancy put together a plate of the roast dinner and dessert for Mrs Bridges, and then they were off. "What's she like," Bethany wanted to know.

"You'll see," Hunter told her, glancing sideways. "She'll appreciate that basket of goodies, that's for sure." His eyes back on the road ahead, Hunter slipped a hand into Bethany's. It felt good to have him hold her hand. It helped confirm she mattered to him. She reflected it had been a long time since someone had cared for her. But never like this. Her parents had cared for her, but with Hunter it was a different sort of caring.

At least she hoped it was. His actions seemed to prove that. "We're almost there," he said out of the blue, and Bethany braced for the sudden stop. "That's it up ahead."

Bethany stared at the rundown cottage and wondered how long it had been since someone had cared enough to carry out repairs on the place. "Looks like it needs a lot of work." She stared at Hunter. It seemed he did what he could, but he also had a job to do. He couldn't spend all his time here.

"The place needs to be demolished. I've tried time and again to get her to move into town." He climbed down from the buggy then helped Bethany down. She glanced at him momentarily then turned away. If she stared at him long enough, she knew what would happen – she'd want to kiss him. They weren't there for that. The dear sweet lady needed their help.

Suddenly the front door flew open. "Git off my land!" Her arms flew all about and she looked angry. Surely this couldn't be the dear lady Hunter had spoken about? "Go on, git." She was suddenly out of the house, heading straight toward Hunter.

She was thin and fragile looking, and quite short – not even five foot in her estimation. At one time she would have been beautiful Bethany was certain, but now she was wrinkled due to her age, and her hair went every which way. She looked like she needed a good meal. Lots of good meals in fact.

In spite of all that, Bethany was terrified of what might happen next.

When she glanced across at him, Hunter was grinning. "Nice to see you too, Mrs Bridges."

She continued toward him and suddenly put her arms around him and hugged him tight. "Good to see you, boy," she said, emotion in her voice. "I thought you weren't comin' back. I could have been dead for all you knew." When she pulled back, she had a smile on her face, but the smile suddenly disappeared when she spotted Bethany. "Who's this you done brought with you without my permission?"

Bethany drew in a breath and stepped back. Perhaps she should have stayed home like Hunter had said. "Mrs Bridges, this is Bethany. She's a…friend."

"Dang it, boy. How many times I gotta tell you to call me Nellie? Or Aunt Nellie if you must?"

She stared at Bethany, then stepped toward her. She suddenly leapt forward and hugged her tight. "Friend? Ha!" She continued hugging Bethany then whispered in her ear. "Don't take no nonsense from this one. He can be hard to git along with." After her initial apprehension, Bethany was grinning. She already like the woman.

"Let's git inside out of the cold," she said. "Bring some of that firewood, will ya, boy?" She winked at Bethany. "Might as well make use of him, now he's here." She went straight to the stove and refilled the kettle from a pail of water she had near the sink. "No runnin' water here, gal," she said. "I git me water from the stream."

Bethany gasped. The stream was so far from here. Mrs Bridges tapped on the window as though she'd read Bethany's mind. "There 'tis. Ain't far, and the water is good an' clean. Not like down in the town."

Hunter arrived with an armful of wood and began to light the fire. "Why didn't you light this earlier? It's freezing in here."

The old lady glanced at Bethany and grinned. "Why would I do that when I knew you'd be here to carry the wood and light the fire."

"How did you know…?" He looked confused.

"Dang it, boy. You're predictable. Every second Sunday you come 'ere, without fail." She filled three mugs with coffee, then waited for the kettle to boil. She turned to Bethany. "Dang fool doesn't even know what he does." It took all her effort for Bethany to not break down laughing.

"I brought something for you," Bethany suddenly said. "I'll go get it from the buggy."

"Stay 'ere with me," Nellie said gently. "Hunter can get it. He's big and strong." It was the first time she'd heard the older woman use his name. She was beginning to wonder if she'd forgotten it. "He's been good to me, that boy," she said with a grin. "The rest of them townies have forgot all 'bout me, I'm sure. But not that boy."

"I'm sure they haven't," Bethany said, not convinced herself. "It's so cold up here, and you must get lonely."

"That I do," Nellie said sadly. "Much as I tease that boy, I enjoy the company." She waved her hands about. "It does get lonely, for certain. But I git nowhere else t' go."

The kettle boiled and Nellie went to pick it up. "Let me," Bethany said, and Nellie let her. She placed the mugs on the table, and the two women sat down. Soon after, Hunter arrived with Bethany's basket of goodies.

"For me?" Nellie said with emotion in her voice when she was handed the basket. "No one ever gives me anythin'."

Hunter rolled his eyes. "What about the time I bought you a jar of coffee?"

"You only done that so you could have coffee," she said dismissing him. "Sit down an' drink."

Nellie pulled each item out of the basket, one by one, then leaned in and breathed in the aroma of the food. "You make these?" she asked Bethany.

"She's a baker, Nellie," Hunter said.

She stared at him. "Finally when I'm on me last legs, he calls me Nellie. Wonders will never cease!"

"Better hang on 't this one, boy," she said, reaching into the basket again. She lifted out the scented soaps and breathed them in. "I haven't had somethin' so special for a very long time." Tears formed in her eyes, and she reached for Bethany. "Yer a kind gal, that's fer sure," she said then pulled out the other items. "Tis all too much for an old bird like me."

She pulled the gloves onto her hands and wrapped the scarf around her neck. The lap blanket landed right where it was meant to be. "Thank ye, gal. Ye didn't have ta do this." She stood and hugged Bethany tight, tears rolling down her cheeks. "Don't let this one slip out yer fingers, boy. She's far too good 't lose." She glanced at Bethany. "Far too good for the likes of you as well."

After their coffee, Hunter had gone around the cottage and fixed all the holes he could find, and anything else that needed doing urgently. He would have to bring far more wood with him next time, he told her.

Bethany saw a totally different side to Hunter today, one she'd never seen before. She had always known he was kind, although it had taken a while for her to see that side of him. But today he'd shown a very special part of himself. And she loved him even more because of it.

Chapter Nine

"You both look knackered," Nancy told them when they finally arrived back to the boarding house. Darkness was already surrounding them and it was time for supper. "Sit yourself down next to the fire, Hunter," she directed him, despite his protests.

Somehow it had become normal for him to eat with everyone else. That wasn't the way he'd planned it, but he wouldn't complain. Anything that meant he got to spend time with Bethany was fine by him.

Bethany glanced from one to the other. "I need to tidy up before supper," she said, pushing at her wayward hair.

Hunter suddenly stood. "I probably look a mess too."

Nancy studied him. "You're not too bad, but you can clean up out back in the laundry. That old cabin ought to be destroyed and old Mrs Bridges forced into town," she said, clearly annoyed. "You put far too much time into fixing the unfixable."

"I know," he said, shrugging his shoulders. "I'd love for her to move into town, but she simply refuses."

"Hmph!" Nancy stared at him. "Off you go then."

As he walked through the kitchen to the laundry, Hunter took in the various aromas. There were two pies sitting on the bench, and vegetables on the stove. He squatted down and could see what looked like cherry cobbler in the oven.

Nancy came up behind him with a towel, and flicked it at him. "Go on, get and clean up," she said laughing, then tossed the towel toward him. "Supper won't be long."

By the time he returned to the sitting room, Bethany was relaxing in one of the comfortable chairs. She looked a little more relaxed. He knew she was concerned about Mrs Bridges, because she'd told him so. If only they could convince her to move into town. Her answer was always the same – it had been her home since she married her dear Ralph. Their five children had been conceived and born there, with only three surviving. They were all gone now, and she was the only one left. If she left, it would feel like she was dismissing a lifetime of memories.

It made his heart ache. She'd become like a grandmother to him over the years. Nellie Bridges had her strange ways, but she was special and he looked forward to visiting her every fortnight. Bethany said she was already looking forward to returning. She'd taken a real shine to the dear old lady, and visa versa.

"You look far better," Nancy told him. "Supper's ready everyone. Sit down." Once seated, she turned to Hunter. "Would you say the blessing, Marshal? You did it so well last time."

He glanced around the table. No one else volunteered, so after they'd all linked hands he bowed his head. "Bless this food and these people, Lord. We also pray for Nellie Bridges, and ask you to keep her safe. Amen."

"Amen."

"How's she doing, Hunter," Jonas asked as he dished some potato onto his plate.

Mildred stared at him. "Yes, how is she, Hunter. Really?"

He glanced from one to the other. "She's faring alright, but would be far better if she lived in town. It is far too cold up in the hills, and the house is a wreck. I've repaired what I could today, but it will take a lot more work to make it truly livable." It saddened him to think of her up there alone. At least she had meals to get her through a few days at least, thanks to Bethany.

Jonas put a hand on Hunter's arm. "You've been going up there regularly for some years now. Let's face it, the cabin should be demolished. You'll get up there one day to find it collapsed on top of her."

Hunter swallowed back emotion. It was true, he knew it was. Short of forcing her to move to town, what could he do? Arrest her? Nellie would never forgive him. Unless he could come up with some sort of plan that made her think it was her idea. But now was not the time.

Bethany stared across the table at him. Her expression said *I know what you're thinking, and I'm thinking it too.* If their ideas aligned, maybe they could pull it off. If they didn't, well, then they'd have to think some more.

"…Thursday. What do you think, Hunter?" Jonas was staring at him, but Hunter hadn't been listening, he'd been lost in his own little world.

"Sorry, I was deep in thought. What was it you said?"

"The tree. You know, for the town center. We usually get it two weeks before Christmas. We're running late this year. A few of us are going Thursday."

"Yeah, sure thing," Hunter said, his mind still ticking over. "Let me know what time you're going, and if I'm available, I'll tag along."

He took a mouthful of Nancy's chicken pie. Bliss. "This is magnificent," he told their hostess, then leaned back and savored the food. It didn't take long before he felt guilty thinking about Nellie Bridges in that rundown shack in the freezing cold. At least he knew she had plenty of food – thanks to Bethany. And also thanks to her, warm hands.

As he took the last mouthful, Nancy came along to collect the soiled dishes, and Lizzie put a mug in front of him. Bethany poured the coffee for everyone.

It was one of the things he loved about this place. It wasn't just a boarding house, it was a community. Everyone who lived here thrived, and he was certain that stubborn old biddy who lived up the mountain would too.

"Nancy," he said quietly. "I need to talk to you later." She stared at him. "It's nothing serious," he said and she nodded before she headed back to the kitchen.

Hunter pulled his coat around himself, and wrapped his scarf around his neck. He pulled on his gloves as he strolled over the road toward Bethany who stood outside the bakery. "I wish I could come with you," she said.

"I know, but it's better this way." He leaned in and kissed her gently. He didn't care who saw, which was a far cry from how he would have felt a few weeks ago.

She reached up and pushed his hat back on his head, then stretched up on her tiptoes and kissed him again. His heart thudded. "Take care," she said, then quickly turned and headed back into the bakery. He stared after her.

He knew she was upset about the situation with Nellie, but it was out of his control. For now anyway.

He climbed up onto the buggy and flicked the reins. As the group of wagons, horses, and buggies pulled out, Hunter knew this assignment could be far more difficult than anything he'd endured before, but it had to be done.

They followed the same path he and Bethany had ridden just days earlier. He'd seen some suitable trees near the turnoff for Nellie's place, and the remainder of the group stopped in a nearby clearing. He alone headed toward the rundown shack. The closer he got, the more hair-brained he decided this scheme was, but he had to try.

Perhaps he should have bought Bethany with him after all.

He slowed the horse down and pulled up outside the cabin. He waited for the door to fly open, and for Nellie to come out screaming for him to get off her land, as she always did in her own silly way.

But she never came.

He sat waiting for several minutes, but still no Nellie. His heart pounded. Was the old lady sick, or worse, dead? He'd left it too late and now regretted it. He swallowed down the emotion that was building in his throat.

He sprang to the front door and pounded on it. It shattered under his strength, and he pulled the rotted boards out of his way. As he stepped over the threshold, fear overtook him. Fear and regret. "Nellie," he called as he entered, trying to warn her he was there. Silence greeted him and panic set in.

He checked the bedroom, and glanced out the window. Hunter couldn't see her, so he went out the back door, and there she was, sitting on the cold, damp ground. "Don't just stand there," she yelled. "I've broken me ankle. Dang thing."

Swallowing felt like nails tearing at his throat. "How long have you been like this," he asked quietly.

"A couple o' days. Maybe more."

Guilt overwhelmed him. It was cold enough during the day up here on the mountain, but overnight was icy. She'd been out here in the artic weather while he'd been tucked up in his warm bed, completely oblivious.

He glanced toward the small stream that ran through her property, and saw the drag marks where she'd tried to get herself inside. He studied the rotten steps and admonished himself for not noticing them before. If they'd been solid, she might have made it inside.

Hunter removed his jacket and put it around her shivering body.

He squatted down to her level. Nellie's foot was on an awkward angle, so she was likely right. He scouted around for a couple of straight sticks to use as splints, then bandaged her ankle using a threadbare sheet he'd found inside and tore up, much to Nellie's disgust. Once done he lifted the frail woman and took her inside, then covered her with a blanket. "Tell me what you need," he said. "I'm taking you to town until you heal."

She glared at him. "Over my dead body."

"If that's how it has to be..." he said, letting his words hang.

He began to rummage through the cottage, throwing her clothes in the same basket Bethany had used to bring her care basket out here last Sunday. "What else do you want?" He studied her. There were no second chances here. Everything she wanted needed to come with them.

"Them things your gal brought for me – the scarf and lap rug. I'm wearing them gloves. Oh, and that special soap." She glared at him. "Since yer forcin' me." He pressed himself not to laugh.

As tragic as it was, this was probably the best thing that had happened. She had to leave to get medical treatment.

"What're ye doing here today anyhow? It can't be Sunday yit?" She suddenly looked confused.

"It's Thursday. Some of the town's men are at your turnoff cutting down a tree for the town center's Christmas tree."

She frowned. "They still doin' that nonsense? The last time I went to the tree ceremony was about twenty years ago," she said. "With my Ralph." She seemed to reminisce and a smile crossed her face. Hunter was certain she was thinking of days gone by and the husband she missed dearly. "Hurry up then," she suddenly said. "If ye got everything, let's git going."

"Yes, Ma'am," he said, trying to fight a grin.

He picked her up gently, blanket and all, and carried her out to the buggy. Once he had her settled, he went back for her meagre belongings, and they were soon on their way.

When they arrived back in town, Hunter took Nellie straight to the doctor's office. "It's definitely broke," Doc Shilling said. "You'll need to rest it for at least six weeks and you'll need crutches," he said, handing them to the older woman. He turned to Hunter. "You did a good job with that splint. I'm not changing it."

"I can't git around on them things," Nellie complained. "It's hard enough gittin' around my place as it is."

"Don't worry," Hunter said. "I have an idea." Nellie stared at him suspiciously. Little did she know he had already planned it. As much as the broken ankle was a terrible thing for the elderly woman, it helped ease his mind.

He picked the frail woman up and carried her out to the buggy. "Where you takin' me?" she demanded, still eyeing him with apprehension.

"Not far. We're going to Nancy's. Do you remember Nancy Richter?"

She stared at him through squinting eyes. "Maybe. What are ye up to, boy?"

He flicked the reins and they were soon on their way. "Here we are," he said a short time later. The front door opened and Nancy came out, smiling and excited to see Nellie.

"This is a nice surprise," she said as she greeted them. He'd warned her it needed to appear unscheduled. It was his idea all along to get Nellie here. Hopefully long term, but that would be up to her in the end. It was far too dangerous for her to go back to her cabin as it was now. That had been proven by her injuries.

"Hello Nancy," he said as though he hadn't seen her recently. "I wondered if you might have a room available for Mrs Bridges to stay in until she heals from her broken ankle?"

"Broken ankle!" Nancy was genuinely shocked. "You poor dear. Yes, yes, I do have a spare room. It's on the ground floor too, so that will work out well." Little did Nellie know Bethany had moved upstairs to allow the older lady easier access. "Bring her into the sitting room, Hunter. That's a good man."

He carried the featherweight woman and sat her near the fire.

"Let me get you something. Tea or coffee?"

Nellie glanced up at him. "Strong coffee, thank ye," she said, apparently surprised to be waited on.

Nancy returned with coffee for three as well as a plate of blueberry muffins. "Bethany made these," she said, offering the muffins to Nellie.

"She's a nice girl, that one. Why she'd 'ave eyes for this one, I'll never know," she said half joking.

It wasn't long before Jonas and Mildred joined them, and Nellie was soon chatting as though they were old friends – just as he'd suspected she would. It had been obvious for a very long time she craved company, but for whatever reason, refused to leave her cabin. If she would agree to stay after she healed, he would go to the cabin and collect the rest of her belongs, meagre as they were.

As he drank his coffee, Hunter was filled with joy. He had tried for so long to get the dear lady into town. It was a shame it took a catastrophe to make it happen, but he was beyond ecstatic she was now safe and warm. If he knew Nancy, she would have plenty of meat on her bones soon too.

Nellie sat on the chair Bethany had placed in the town center for her. She said she hadn't witnessed the raising of the tree for decades, and it would be a first for Bethany too. They sat side by side and waited in anticipation. Nellie reached over and took the younger woman's hand. "Thank ye for organizing for me to come 'ere," she said quietly.

"It was all Hunter. I just supplied the chairs."

"That boy doesn't deserve you," she said, ignoring Bethany's words. She had a real soft spot for the dear old lady who felt more like a grandmother to her.

"Are you looking forward to Christmas luncheon tomorrow?"

Nellie stared ahead. "We used to have wonderful Christmases when the children were small. Not so much after Ralph passed."

Bethany squeezed Nellie's hand as a tear rolled down the old lady's face. She swiped at her cheeks then turned to Bethany. "Memories," she said quietly. "They can be good, but also painful."

It broke her heart to see Nellie like this.

As the tree was finally lifted to a standing position after nearly an hour of ropes being tied to branches, there was much delight from the townsfolk. As soon as it was secured in place, people moved forward and added their handmade decorations. "Perhaps next year, we can do that too," Bethany told her. "We have a year to work on it."

"Tradition says newlyweds make a decoration between them, then add it each year thereafter," Nellie told her pointedly.

The heat rose in Bethany's face.

"That boy needs to git and ask you to marry him!"

Bethany didn't know how to answer that, so she didn't. Instead she watched as Hunter and the other men ensured the tree was properly secured.

What would it be like being married to Hunter, she wondered, and her heart exploded.

Chapter Ten

Everyone sat around the dining room table, including Nellie. She'd been reluctant to join, saying she was an outsider. Everyone quickly dispersed that notion.

So there she sat, eyes wide at the array of food strewn across the elegantly decorated table. Both Bethany and Nancy had been up since dawn preparing the food, both enjoying themselves. Yes, it was hard work, but when you loved to cook as they did, it wasn't work. Not really.

The decorated Christmas cake sat in the center of the table, and large bowls of carrots, turnips, parsnips and green beans were placed along the white cloth. They would be passed around when the time came. There was a jug of gravy and also a bowl of cranberry sauce on each end of the long table, and bowls of nuts sat there too.

A large leg of ham, and a piece of pork took pride of place. Everyone watched as Hunter carved the meat.

The pudding was bubbling away on the stove, and would be ready by the time they finished eating the main course. She would make custard to accompany it, and Nancy also had cream for those who preferred it.

Nellie sat next to Bethany, and held her hand tight when it came time for Hunter to say the blessing. "Thank you Lord for this abundance of food we are sharing today as we celebrate Jesus' birth, and for all the greatness you have brought into our lives. Thank you also for bringing Nellie safely to us. Amen."

"Amen."

When Bethany looked up, tears filled Nellie's eyes. "Thank ye, boy," she said, emotion in her voice. "I want to give yer a big hug, but I cannit cause of this broken ankle." Hunter stood and came around the table and hugged her tight.

Silence surrounded them, and Bethany was certain everyone felt the same sort of emotion she was feeling right now.

"Go on, git now and eat your food." Hunter grinned, and the atmosphere suddenly became festive.

The table was cleared of all the soiled dishes, and Bethany carried in the huge pudding she'd made. Nancy carried the custard and cream. Gasps surrounded them as they entered.

This time it was Bethany who cut the pudding and dished it out to everyone.

"This is delicious."

"You're a wonderful cook, Bethany."

"So good."

Lots of praise surrounded her. Hunter stared at her, a grin on his face. "You're a pretty good cook, I guess," he said as he chuckled.

She knew he was joking but threw the kitchen towel at him anyway. "Tuck in, everyone," she said, then took her place at the table. She picked up her spoon and took a mouthful. It was good. Perhaps the best she'd ever made.

When everyone finished eating, she announced they could have seconds, since there was plenty left over. Hunter took up the offer, as she knew he would. She was beyond full, and refrained. Bethany was pleased to see Nellie had eaten her fill. It was heartwarming to know she would now be looked after. For the rest of her life if she agreed.

When everyone had eaten their fill, they moved into the sitting room while Nancy, Bethany, and Mildred tidied up and did the dishes. Once done, they joined the others.

Hunter studied her as she sat down on one of the comfortable chairs. As she leaned back her eyes began to flutter closed. She'd been up for hours, but that was nothing new. Catering for so many on such a big occasion had taken a lot out of her.

When she opened her eyes again, everyone was staring at her. Hunter suddenly stood, and they followed his every movement. She wondered what was going on. Suddenly he was down on one knee, and his gaze never left her face.

"Bethany Lancaster," he said, and she swallowed down the lump in her throat. "We didn't get off to a great start, but over time I've grown to love you." She could hear the emotion in his voice. "Will you marry me?"

Tears pooled in her eyes. Silence surrounded them as everyone waited for her response. She reached out with a shaking hand and cupped his cheek. "You were an absolute pain when we first met," she said, her voice shaky. "But I too, have grown to love you."

He covered her hand with his own and gazed at her.

"Are you goin' t' marry 'im or not?" Nellie said impatiently.

She couldn't help but laugh, no matter how nervous she was feeling. "Yes, I'll marry you," she said. Hunter was suddenly off the floor and pulled her out of the chair. Before she knew what was happening he was kissing her. She didn't care who was watching.

~*~

The wedding happened far more quickly than Bethany had anticipated.

Three weeks after Christmas she stood at the back of the church. She'd ordered a new gown for the occasion. It was made of a soft pink silk, and had a rounded neckline. It was high enough to be decent, but didn't tug at her throat. The bodice was ruffled down to her waist, and the top of the sleeves were the same at the top, and were then straight down to her wrists. Coming in at the waist, it was then straight all the way to the ankle. A matching hat sat on the side of her head.

Her outfit was perfect for today's ceremony, but by adding a brooch or other embellishment, it would be suitable for any special occasions they attended in the future.

As she stared down the aisle toward her soon-to-be husband, she thought about fate. She knew if the stagecoach hadn't been robbed, she probably would have continued on to the next town.

What a tragedy that would have been.

Nellie stood next to her, also in a new gown, leaning on the crutches she'd vowed to master when Bethany asked her to give her away. She'd become far more than a friend to the pair, and was more like a surrogate grandmother. Even more than she was before.

She'd settled into the boarding house, and with each passing day, she looked far healthier, which was pleasing to both Bethany and Hunter. She'd already said she wanted to stay on, which was even better.

The organ music began to play, and Pastor Kelly stood at the altar with Hunter. The church was filled with locals despite their plans for a simple and private ceremony. The townsfolk were all eager to see their marshal married off, they'd told her on more than one occasion.

"Dearly Beloved, we are gathered here today," the pastor said after Nellie had offered her to Hunter.

She didn't hear much more of the ceremony. Instead she studied Hunter for most of the time. In fact she hadn't realized it was over until Hunter grabbed her and kissed her like he'd never kissed her before.

When they left the church, rice was thrown at them from every direction. It was down Bethany's back, down her front, and in her hair to the point she was itching. "Come with me," Hunter said, dragging her away. "We'll be back for the wedding breakfast," he told Martha Greenwood who had arranged it for him.

"Where are we going?" Bethany was confused. She had no idea where Hunter was taking her. Until they arrived.

The marshal's house sat not far from the jailhouse. She'd never been inside since that would be improper. But now they were married, that all changed. He unlocked the door and picked her up, then carried her across the threshold, kicking the front door closed. He stole a kiss as he carried her to the bedroom. Only then did he place her on the floor.

"Let me get that terrible gown off you," he said. "We'll get rid of all that awful rice." And that's exactly what he did.

Epilogue

Two years later…

"I truly love this place, Hunter," Bethany told him as they went for their daily stroll around town. "When I first came here I had a bad feeling about it." She glanced up at him. If she knew anything about her husband, she knew he loved the tiny town of Alsburgh.

"I don't blame you. You had a shocking introduction to the place." He reached out and stroked her cheek. "I'm glad you decided to stay though. We would never had met otherwise."

"If I'd had the choice, I never would have stayed. I had no money, remember?" He nodded. "If you hadn't paid for my board at Nancy's I have no idea what I would have done." She got up on her toes and kissed his cheek.

She glanced up at the Christmas tree sitting in the town square. "I love this tradition," she said. "I look forward to it every year." She knew Hunter did too.

He held her hand and they turned the corner toward home. "I'm really tired," Bethany said. "I need to rest for a few minutes."

Hunter unlocked the door and ushered her through. He put their son on the floor and he took off in a hurry.

"Luke Benjamin, don't you dare!" Bethany ran across the room toward their fifteen-month-old son and the Christmas tree. Well, as best she could with her swollen belly.

Hunter frowned. "What have I told you, young man?" He scooped the boy up and cuddled him. "We don't touch the tree, remember." Luke's eyes filled with tears and Hunter patted his back. "It's alright," he said gently. "Just don't do it again."

He headed toward Bethany who was panting. "You don't look good. Come and sit down." He led her to a comfortable chair, then made her a cup of tea.

"I'll go and get Nellie. I'm sure she'll be happy to mind Luke for a while."

"No, don't, I'm fine. It just took the wind out of me, that's all." She took another sip of her tea. "It's time for his nap anyway."

When Hunter came back from putting the boy down for his nap, he sat down beside her. "What can I do for you? Should I get Doc Shilling?"

She smiled up at him. "I'm not due for a couple more weeks. I'm sure I'll be fine."

"Nellie told me she's happy to move in to look after Luke if you want."

"Please don't uproot her, Hunter," she said, pleading with him. "You know how hard it was to get her into town. Let her stay where she loves."

Of course he agreed.

She sat back into the chair and closed her eyes. After a few minutes she opened them again. She wasn't at all comfortable, so stood.

"Where are you off to now?"

Hunter's concern was heartwarming, but unwarranted. "I'm just going to lay down for a while." Before she had a chance to go any further, he'd scooped her up and carried her to the bedroom.

Pulling back the covers, he laid her down and pulled off her shoes, then covered her up. "You can go back to work now," she said, as her eyes began to flutter closed.

"I'm not needed," he said, leaning in to kiss her cheek. "I have two deputies who are more than capable."

He laid down on the bed next to her, and faced her. "I love you more than life itself," he said as he stroked her cheek.

"I love you too," she said, feeling his love fill her whole being. "I never want to be without you. I am so glad we met, even if it was amidst tragedy." She shivered. "Hold me," she said, and he did.

She never intended to let him go, and thanked God for bringing Hunter to her.

The End

Bethany's Christmas Pudding Recipe

This recipe has been passed down through my husband's family for generations, and is the kind of pudding your great-great grandmother would have made – wrapped in a clean calico cloth and boiled for hours on end. I can still recall our puddings hanging from the beams in the kitchen after our family Christmas baking days each year. The wonderful fragrances that lingered for days, if not weeks – not to forget the hard work my mother, aunties and other relatives put in to make the day a success.

The thick white outer coating is what sets this pudding apart from the rest. (And it doesn't need to be hung from the rafters!)

The pudding can be cooked several months ahead and frozen – in the cloth - or alternatively you can make it one week ahead of time. To reheat ready for eating, boil for a short time on the day of use. You can also cut into individual slices and reheated in the microwave.

For best results, butter should be used where indicated, not margarine. (It keeps far longer too.)

Ingredients:

3 lbs (9 cups or 1.5 kg) Mixed Fruit

1/4 Pint (1/2 cup or 4 oz) Fresh Orange Juice

1 lb (500 grams) Butter

1 lb (2 cups) Brown Sugar

8 Eggs

2 Green Apples (such as Granny Smith's) – Grated

1 cup Plain Flour

Pinch Salt

1 cup Soft Fresh Breadcrumbs

1 teaspoon each Nutmeg, Mixed Spice and Cinnamon

Method

In an extra large bowl, soak the fruit in orange juice. Set aside.

In a large bowl, cream the sugar and butter thoroughly, add eggs one at a time, beating well. Add grated apples. Now add sifted flour, salt and spices. Mix well. Add this mixture to the original fruit mix that you previously set aside.   Add breadcrumbs and blend the entire mix thoroughly.

Calico needs to be thoroughly clean before use. If new, prepare by washing ahead of time.

Prepare the calico cloth   (Use only unbleached calico):

Take washed calico, dipped in boiling water, and lay pieces of calico flat on kitchen table and completely cover with sifted plain flour (white only).

Place entire pudding mixture on the cloth (in the center), and tie securely with strong string. Boil in cloth (in boiling water) for approximately five hours. Ensure water stays on the boil the whole time, and top up with boiling water when required.

This recipe makes one extra large pudding, or you can split into four smaller puddings, which reduces the cooking time. To check if cooked, slide a metal skewer down the tiny gap in the top of the pudding where the top is tied.

When cooked, remove from boiling water and allow to cool slightly on a plate. If not using immediately, transfer to fridge after the pudding is cool.

To freeze: Leave in fridge overnight to avoid breakage, then remove cloth and wrap in foil. The pudding is now ready to freeze.

Plum pudding can be served with White Sauce, Custard, Brandy Sauce, Cream, or Ice-cream. Can be served hot or cold.

Brandy Cream

This is my sister's recipe. As far as she's concerned, it's not Christmas without the Brandy Cream. Unfortunately she really loves the Brandy flavor and is often heavy handed.

Ingredients

1/4 cup brandy

300 ml cream, lightly whipped

2 separated eggs

1/2 cup castor sugar

Method

Fold brandy into lightly whipped cream. Put aside.

Beat egg whites until soft peaks form (do not over beat), and gradually add sugar. Beat together until thick and sugar has dissolved.

Gradually add egg yolks. Add brandy and cream mixture and fold into egg mixture.

Store in sealed container in fridge until ready to use. (This recipe is best made the day you intend to use it. We normally make it a few minutes before serving the plum pudding.)

From the Author

Thank you so much for reading my book – I hope you enjoyed it.

I would greatly appreciate you leaving a review where you purchased, even if it is only a one-liner. It helps to have my books more visible!

About the Author

135

Multi-published, award-winning and bestselling author Cheryl Wright, former secretary, debt collector, account manager, writing coach, and shopping tour hostess, loves reading.

She writes historical romantic suspense and historical western romance.

She lives in Melbourne, Australia, and is married with two adult children and has six grandchildren, and twin great-grandchildren.

When she's not writing, she can be found in her craft room making greeting cards.

Links

Website: *http://www.cheryl-wright.com/*

Facebook Reader Group:
https://www.facebook.com/groups/cherylwrightaut hor/

Join My Newsletter:

https://cheryl-wright.com/newsletter/
(and receive a free book)